"I don't like this," Joe said.

"Come on, Wishbone." Joe and Wishone headed back toward the sales counter of the darkened bookstore.

The shelves looked dark and mysterious. Anyone could be lurking in the shadows. Wishbone smelled Joe's nervousness—and then he heard the squeak of a floorboard!

"Come on, Joe! This way!" The brave Jack Russell terrier ran toward the storage room.

"Wishbone!" Joe yelled. "No!"

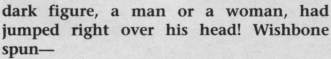

The charging Wishbone paid no attention. "Gangway! Guard dog coming through!" Then Wishbone ducked—a dark figure, a man or a woman, had jumped right over his head! Wishbone spun—

"Hey!" he heard Joe yell. Then came the sound of someone stumbling, crashing!

One thought raced through Wishbone's mind: *Joe's being attacked!*

WISHBONE Mysteries

RIDDLE OF THE WAYWARD BOOKS

by Brad Strickland and Thomas E. Fuller

WISHBONE™ created by Rick Duffield

SCHOLASTIC INC.

New York Toronto London Auckland Sydney
Mexico City New Delhi Hong Kong

ISBN 0-590-37542-3

12 11 10 9 8 7 6 5 4 3 2 1   8 9/9 0 1 2 3/0

Printed in the U.S.A.   40

First Scholastic printing, November 1998

Edited by Kevin Ryan
Copy edited by Jonathon Brodman
Cover concept, design, and interior illustrations by Lyle Miller
Wishbone photograph by Carol Kaelson

To our favorite announcer,
Mr. William L. Brown

FROM THE BIG RED CHAIR . . .

Oh . . . hi! Wishbone here. You caught me right in the middle of some of my favorite things—books. Let me welcome you to my brand-new book series, WISHBONE MYSTERIES. In each story, I help my human friends solve a puzzling mystery. In *RIDDLE OF THE WAYWARD BOOKS*, Joe and I track down a mysterious burglar who breaks into the used-book store where Joe is working for the summer. We soon learn the intruder is interested in more than just stealing books!

This story takes place early in the summer, before the events that you'll see in the second season of my WISHBONE television show. In this story, Joe is thirteen and will start the eighth grade in the fall. Just like me, he's always ready for adventure.

You're in for a real treat, so pull up a chair and a snack and sink your teeth into *RIDDLE OF THE WAYWARD BOOKS*.

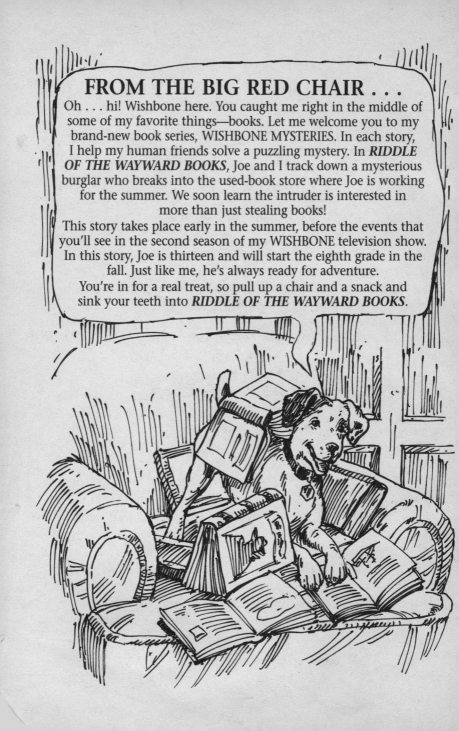

Chapter One

Right after breakfast on Friday, Joe Talbot fought off a feeling of nervousness, pushed back from the kitchen table, and said, "Wish me luck, Mom."

Dark-haired Ellen Talbot smiled at her thirteen-year-old son. "The school year just ended. You'll find a summer job in plenty of time. Don't worry."

He shook his head, and his brown hair fell forward. "All the good ones are taken. Everyone I know has one already. David's helping Ms. Gilmore set up the computer database for the Oakdale Historical Society, and Sam's working for her dad at Pepper Pete's. She's been there a lot since Mr. Kepler bought the pizza parlor. Anyway, I'm pretty late. Why did I have to come down with the flu last week?"

"Well, you're over it now," Ellen said as she walked Joe to the front door. "Go get 'em!"

Joe grinned and called, "Come on, Wishbone!"

Joe's best friend, a white-with-brown-spots Jack Russell terrier, came running. Joe and Wishbone left the house and walked to the center of Oakdale. They went up and down the streets, stopping everywhere— the radio station, the movie theater, the antiques store, the grocery store. The answer was always the same: "Sorry, son, we don't need any more help right now."

Joe walked dejectedly up Main Street. Wishbone fell in step next to him. Joe was getting discouraged, and to him, even Wishbone looked as if he were feeling low.

"I guess we could just head on home, Wishbone." Joe sighed as they trudged along. "But Mom's at the library, and David and Sam are at work."

Wishbone panted as he trotted beside Joe. He looked up with what Joe took to be a sympathetic glance.

Joe sighed again. "I mean, we've already checked out just about every place I can think of!"

Wishbone barked.

Joe shrugged. "Guess we just have to keep looking."

At that moment, Wishbone stopped and sat in the doorway of a shop. Joe walked on a couple of steps before turning around and looking back at Wishbone.

"What is it, boy?"

Wishbone stared at the shop. Joe came over and took a look, too. The window held a collection of stuffed animals, porcelain figurines, toys, and books. Faded gold letters on the window spelled out the words ROSIE'S RENDEZVOUS BOOKS & GIFTS. In the corner of the window was a neat, handwritten sign:

WANTED:
Industrious, hardworking young person
with a love of books to assist in inventory and
shelving. Flexible hours. Modest salary.
Please see proprietor, K. J. Gurney.

Joe read the sign twice, and he felt his hopes rise. "Okay, boy, this just might be what I'm looking for. You wait right here."

With a deep doggie sigh, Wishbone settled down under the shade of a tree on the sidewalk and rested his jaw on his paws. A little bell rang as Joe opened the door, went inside, and marched over to the check-out counter. A couple of clerks were working in the store. Joe approached one he knew, Mary Benson.

"Hi," he said, feeling nervous.

With a smile, Mary replied, "Hi, Joe. May I help you?"

Joe cleared his throat, fighting off the feeling of butterflies fluttering in his stomach. "I'm . . . I'm here about the job."

"Job?" Mary frowned. "I don't think we have any—Oh, the one advertised in the window? That isn't for the gift shop. That would be for Mr. Gurney, upstairs in the used-book store. Just go to the back of the shop and up the stairs."

9

"Oh," Joe said. "Thanks."

Mary gave him an encouraging smile. "Good luck."

Joe walked past rows of shelves filled with every kind of gift imaginable until he came to an elegant old wooden staircase. Although Joe had often been in Rosie's Rendezvous before, he had never gone upstairs. He had heard of the bookstore on the second floor, but he had never explored it. *Probably,* he thought, *it's a dusty little attic with a few old books.* He climbed up the steps until he came to a door with a carved wooden plaque that proudly proclaimed RENDEZVOUS BOOKS. PLEASE COME IN. So he did— and he stood gaping in the doorway.

In front of him, in all directions, stretched row after row of bookcases crammed with books. There were paperbacks, huge leather-bound volumes, best sellers, and—in glass cases—some books that looked quite old and valuable. "Wow!" Joe said breathlessly, looking around. "It's like a library!"

"Except that when you check these books out, you get to keep them," replied a jolly voice.

Joe turned and looked for the voice. He found himself staring at an elderly man in a blue suit with a checkered vest. He had a trim white beard. The way he wore his glasses—tilted up so the lenses were lost in his unruly nest of white hair—made him look like an absent-minded Santa Claus. The man stood behind an old-fashioned brass cash register that sat atop a counter. He leaned across to shake Joe's hand.

"Kilgore J. Gurney, bookseller extraordinaire, at your service. What may I do for you?"

With more butterflies fluttering in his stomach, Joe said, "I've come about the job, sir."

For a moment, Mr. Gurney looked completely puzzled. "Job? What— Oh, the ad in the window! I'd almost forgotten. Well, you're obviously young. I assume you are also industrious, hardworking, and have a love of books?" Mr. Gurney's eyes twinkled, as if he were on the verge of bursting out with a hearty laugh.

Joe had to grin. "Well, my mom says so."

"An excellent reference! What's your name? It's always easier to talk to my employees when I know their names."

Joe stared at the beaming Mr. Gurney for a moment. "*Employees?* Do you mean I have the job?"

Mr. Gurney chuckled and stroked his beard. "Only if you have a name. I'm afraid I'm always rather strict about that."

"Yes, sir! My name's Joe Talbot."

Mr. Gurney raised his bushy eyebrows. "Talbot? Is your mother Ellen Talbot, by any chance?"

"Yes, sir."

Mr. Gurney's laugh was deep and rumbling. "A librarian's son! Wonderful! Welcome to Rendezvous Books, Mr. Joe Talbot. Let me introduce you to your duties." He searched on a shelf below the counter until he retrieved a jangling key ring.

Then Joe followed Mr. Gurney through the tall stacks of what looked like used books. Windows on one wall let the morning sunlight filter in. Old armchairs were clustered in groups between the shelves. In many of them, people sat reading. They nodded absently to Mr. Gurney and Joe as they walked by. Mr. Gurney sorted through his keys as he and Joe approached a door with a frosted-glass window. The bearded man unlocked the door and swung it open.

"Behold! Welcome to your new place of gainful employment, Joe!"

Mr. Gurney gestured grandly around the cluttered

area. Shelves jammed the walls of this room, but boxes and stacks of books took up most of the floor space.

"I've bought several large private collections lately, and Juvenalia is a bit of a mess. This is my storage-and-inventory room, too, and there's lots to sort out."

The word puzzled Joe. He asked, "Juven-*what?*"

Stepping over and around cardboard cartons, Mr. Gurney said, "Juvenalia, Joe. It's a category of books that refers to the works of authors that they wrote when they were young, or books by authors written for young readers. They all have to be shelved by author, series, and title— oh, and also by condition. That's very important in the used-book business—condition. The better a book's condition, the more valuable it is, and collectors pay good prices for volumes in top-quality shape."

Joe examined the pile of boxes closest to the door. They were filled to the top with books wrapped in brightly colored dust jackets. He picked up one and stared at a picture of a fierce, muscular man in a loincloth, brandishing a long knife. Across the top of the jacket was emblazoned *Tarzan and the Leopard Men.*

Joe felt excited at the find. "Wow! Tarzan was in a book?"

Mr. Gurney took the volume from him and looked down at it fondly. "Tarzan was in many books, Joe, all by the great writer Edgar Rice Burroughs. If you like Tarzan, you'd probably enjoy reading *Bomba the Jungle Boy,* and *The Lone Ranger,* and *Tom Corbett,* and . . ."

Mr. Gurney practically danced around the room in a cloud of book dust, snatching volumes from boxes and shelves and stacking them in Joe's arms.

"This is what kids read before television was invented, back when it cost a quarter to go to a movie, and popcorn was a dime, and sodas a nickel. I have a million rainy afternoons and flash-lit nights on my shelves, a hundred thousand adventures and thrills and cliffhangers. And every single one of them has to be catalogued and shelved. Still want the job?"

Joe struggled to arrange the stack of books he held so that he wouldn't drop any. "Yes, sir! I had no idea Rosie's Rendezvous had a used-book store upstairs."

Mr. Gurney sighed. "Many people don't. Come downstairs to Rosie's, and we'll pop open a soda to celebrate your hiring."

Back downstairs, Mr. Gurney fed some coins into an old-fashioned red soda machine, twisted a gray lever, and removed two icy bottles. After opening the sodas, Joe's new boss raised the glistening bottle to his lips and drained half of it with one gulp.

"My, I do like drinking out of these old bottles—the soda just tastes better to me. By the way, Joe, did you notice that there's a little dog doing backflips outside the front door?"

"Wishbone!" Joe cried, and he raced for the door.

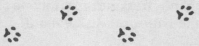

Wishbone was happy to dart inside the moment the door opened. "It's about time you remembered the faithful dog! Hey, Joe, did you get the job? Give a dog a clue, will you?"

Joe stooped and grabbed Wishbone's collar. "Shush, Wishbone! You have to be quiet in here, boy."

"Quiet?" Wishbone radiated indignation. "I'm not a quiet-type dog! Jack Russell terriers are very expressive!"

Mr. Gurney came over and squatted down next to Joe. "Ah, then this fine, intelligent canine is yours, my boy?"

Wishbone gazed up at the kindly looking bearded

man. "Fine intelligent canine? Whoa! Who is this observant guy, Joe? He has excellent taste."

Joe said, "This is Wishbone, Mr. Gurney."

"A very great pleasure, Mr. Bone." Mr. Gurney held out his hand. "Kilgore J. Gurney, at your service."

Shaking hands was one of Wishbone's best tricks. He seemed to smile with pride as he did it. "Joe, this guy is very polite, too."

"Smart fellow." Mr. Gurney stood up. "However, such an intelligent animal might be bored by having to stay indoors all day, so perhaps he'd be better off if he stayed at home."

Wishbone could hardly believe his floppy ears. "Stay home? You're already losing points, Mr. G.!"

"Have you been selling books for a long time, Mr. Gurney?" Joe asked.

The elderly man smiled. "All my life, my boy. My mother, Rose Gurney, opened this gift shop back in the 1940s, and my father, Henry Gurney, ran the Oakdale

14

College bookstore for years. I got my love of books from them—you might say it's in my blood. Cut me, and I bleed ink! X-ray me, and you'll see that my insides are made of dusty novels and flashy paperbacks! When I sold Rosie's Rendezvous to the current owners, I kept the top floor for my bookshop. Now, if we agree on a salary, can you start today?"

"Yes, sir. Should I take Wishbone home first?"

Wishbone looked up, giving Mr. Gurney the "Great Big Puppy Eyes" look. "Please let me stay! Oh, please, please, please!"

Mr. Gurney smiled and shook his head. "There's no need, as long as he stays upstairs and is quiet. Come with me, Joe, and I'll give you some reading material."

Wishbone and Joe followed as Mr. Gurney hurried upstairs. First Mr. Gurney showed them through the entire store, pointing out various sections of books. It was a comfortable place, with armchairs scattered around, and in one nook, a dusty stuffed parrot sat on a perch. Across from the sales counter were two rooms. One was for storage, processing, and children's books. The other was a messy office, with paperwork and books piled everywhere. Mr. Gurney offered a salary that seemed good, and Joe agreed to it at once. After rummaging in a file cabinet for a fat expanding folder, Joe's new boss told him to sit at a table near the cashier's counter.

Mr. Gurney plopped the bulging folder onto the table. "Here is a little something I put together to help my employees understand how to evaluate old books. Take it home with you tonight and study it."

"I'll read every bit of what's in here, Mr. Gurney. You can count on me!"

"I'm sure I can, Joe, I'm sure I can."

Wishbone grinned a big doggie grin. "Yes! And you can count on me, too, Mr. Gurney! Just call me 'abacus'!"

Joe sat and read for a couple of hours, and Wishbone lay quietly next to him. Every once in a while, Joe would read something aloud to Wishbone—about old books, first editions, or rare volumes. Wishbone listened carefully and absorbed everything. The day passed and gradually the customers left the store.

Finally, Mr. Gurney came over to Joe and Wishbone. "Closing time. I'm going to walk around and make sure that no one is so wrapped up in cruising on the *Nautilus* with Captain Nemo or mourning for Little Nell in *The Old Curiosity Shop* that they get locked in. How are you doing, Joe?"

Sounding proud of himself, Joe replied, "Fine, sir! I've read nearly half of what's in the folder."

"First-rate!" Mr. Gurney said. Then he walked away, chuckling.

Wishbone got up from where he had been lying at Joe's feet and trotted down the rows of shelves. "May as well help out! Let's see—nobody here, nobody here, nobody here. . . ."

After a minute, Wishbone heard Joe call him. He raced back. Mr. Gurney was holding the door open, but he clapped his hand to his forehead. "Oh, my stars! I'll lose my head next. Joe, I've got to bring some new purchases in from my car. Would you mind waiting here? If any customers come up, tell them we're closed."

"Sure," Joe said.

"Thanks. I'll be back in a flash."

Mr. Gurney left, and Wishbone sat a Joe's feet, panting happily. "Well, Joe, this is a great job— What's that?" He jerked his head around, ears perked and alert. He had heard a noise.

"What's wrong, fella?" Joe asked.

Wishbone got to his feet, the fur on his neck

bristling. He sniffed and stared down an aisle, toward the storage and processing room. "Someone's there, Joe! Someone sneaky!"

"What's the—" Joe stood up. "I heard something."

"Me, too! I'll check it out!" Wishbone stalked away.

"Wishbone!" Joe hurried behind him.

It was dark between all the rows of tall shelves. Wishbone sniffed, but so many people had been in and out of the store that his nose couldn't tell him much. "Hmm . . . I wonder where the sneaky person went." His ears perked up at the soft scuffle of a footstep.

Joe paused right behind Wishbone. "Who's there?" he called out. No answer. Louder, in a shaky voice, Joe yelled, "Is anybody up here?" As if in answer, the overhead lights clicked off. Wishbone heard Joe swallow hard. "I don't like this," Joe muttered. "Come on, boy." They headed toward the sales counter.

At that moment, a cloud drifted across the sun, and the light coming through the distant windows suddenly dimmed noticeably. All at once the shelves of books became dark, mysterious. Anyone could be lurking in the shadows.

Wishbone smelled his friend's nervousness—and then he heard the squeak of a floorboard! "Come on, Joe! This way!" The brave Jack Russell terrier ran toward the storage room.

"Wishbone!" yelled Joe. "No!"

The charging Wishbone paid no attention. "Gangway! Guard dog coming through!" Then he ducked—a dark figure jumped right over his head! Wishbone spun around.

"Hey!" he heard Joe yell. Then he heard the sound of stumbling, crashing!

One thought raced through Wishbone's mind: *Joe's being attacked!*

17

Chapter Two

Joe had no time to react. A dark figure raced out of the shadows, shoved him, and rushed past. Joe stumbled against a shelf, knocking a few volumes off.

Instantly, Wishbone charged down the aisle, growling. Joe heard the door to the shop open and then slam closed. Footsteps clattered on the staircase, and then came silence. He turned the lights back on. Wishbone sniffed at the door, snarling.

"It's okay," Joe said, his heart still pounding from surprise. "The person is gone, boy. I'm all right."

Leaving Wishbone to guard the door, a nervous Joe went to pick up the fallen books.

A moment later, Mr. Gurney called out, "Joe! Where are you?"

Joe returned to the sales counter, where Mr. Gurney stood beside a stack of books. Joe's voice was still shaky as he said, "Someone was hiding in the store. I'm pretty sure it was a man. He bumped into me and then ran out."

Mr. Gurney checked the cash register. "Nothing taken. Probably just someone who didn't notice the time. Well, he's gone now. There's no harm done."

But Joe was not convinced. "Why did he run from us?"

Mr. Gurney shrugged. "The important thing is that he's gone."

Wishbone, Mr. Gurney, and Joe locked up and then went downstairs. Rosie's Rendezvous was already closed, its lights out. To Joe, the shop looked strange and different in the dark. Mr. Gurney made sure no one was there, and then they left by a back door that led into an alleyway. Wishbone sniffed around, and Joe swallowed hard. "I think that might have been a burglar up in the shop," he said.

Mr. Gurney clapped his hand on Joe's shoulder. "Don't let it worry you, Joe. That was no monster. Just a customer."

Joe was not so sure. Not so sure at all.

Early that evening, a knock sounded at the door of the Talbot home at 813 Forest Lane. Wishbone launched himself from the big red chair in the downstairs study, where he had definitely not been napping.

"I'll get it! I get it!" He raced through the house. "No problem, it's my job—*I'll get it!*" He reached the front door just in time to see Ellen swing it open. "Unless, of course, you want to, Ellen." Wishbone lay down and dropped his head onto his paws. *No one ever listens to the dog,* he thought.

Ellen held the door open. "Oh, Sam, David. Come on in."

"Thank you, Mrs. Talbot," David Barnes said in his serious voice. David, one of Joe's best friends, really wasn't always serious—he just sounded that way.

"Joe called us, Mrs. Talbot." Sam Kepler made a show of adjusting her baseball cap with the Pepper Pete's emblem on it. "He said he'd finally gotten a job, and we had to come right over and hear all about it!"

Wishbone sat up. "That's right, Sam! Hey, you smell great tonight—just like pepperoni!"

Ellen said, "He's in the study."

Wishbone led the way. "Come on, guys! I'll take you right to him and— Ohh, that feels good!" Sam had stooped to scratch him behind the ears and had found just the right spot. Wishbone shook his head. "Got to remember my duties! Joe and his news first—ear-scratching second. Follow me!"

Joe heard Sam and David coming, and he pretended to be all wrapped up in his reading. He lay on the floor, surrounded by his books, his chin propped on his hands and his eyes riveted on a stack of typewritten pages.

"Gee," Sam said from the doorway. "School's out, you know."

"Yeah," David cut in. "You never studied like that in class. How come you're doing it now?"

"Hi, guys," Joe said, smiling up at them and enjoying their quizzical expressions. "I'm not studying—I'm working!"

Sam flopped into a chair and adjusted her cap. "Looks like studying to me."

Joe rolled over and sat up. "No, seriously, I have an important job over at Rendezvous Books helping Mr. Gurney, the owner, do his book inventory!"

"Hey, great!" David said, beaming. "I knew you'd get some neat job! Mr. Gurney's in the database I'm working on with Ms. Gilmore. He's donated lots of old books to the historical society."

Joe gave David a long look. "You *know* about Rendezvous Books?"

"Doesn't everybody?" asked Sam, scratching Wishbone's ears.

Joe shook his head. "I'd heard about it, but I'd never been there before. It's a neat place."

Sam grinned. "I agree. How come you have to study? Don't you just have to know the alphabet in order to shelve books?"

Joe laughed. "Sure—if you're just *shelving* books. But I'm helping with *inventory,* and with inventory you have to know the *condition* of the books, too." He stood up and walked over to a bookcase, pulled a book out, looked at it critically, and held it up. "For instance," he proclaimed in his best I'm-the-teacher voice, "this particular book is foxed."

David reached for the book. "Which means?"

Joe explained, "Foxing is what happens when the paper is discolored or spotted with brown stains that look like rust."

David raised his eyebrows. "Uh . . . paper doesn't rust, Joe."

Pointing to some dark patches, Joe replied, "I know—but it *looks* like rust. It's caused by chemical impurities in the paper."

David took the book and stared at the indicated spots. "Cool. I'll bet there's a science experiment that I could do, based on this."

Sam stretched her neck to look over David's shoulder as he turned the pages. "Gee, there's more to old books than I thought."

Joe was happy to see her take an interest in his new work. "There's more than *I* thought! Wait until I tell you about the Tarzan books."

21

Sam looked over at Joe, her eyes wide. "Tarzan was in a book?"

Joe started to explain to his attentive friends about the wonderful treasures Mr. Gurney had shown him at Rendezvous Books. Then he trailed off, uncertain of whether to talk about what had happened at the end of the day. He bit his lip and said, "The only problem I had was that a burglar might have come into the shop today."

Sam looked up from a scruffy copy of Jules Verne's *Journey to the Center of the Earth*. "A burglar?" she echoed.

"Well . . . maybe." Joe told his friends about the incident with the shadowy figure.

David whistled. "Maybe you'd better take Wishbone to work with you," he suggested. "Rendezvous Books might need a watchdog!"

Wishbone sat up suddenly, looking as if he entirely agreed.

What a great day! Joe thought the next morning as he raced down the bike path into the main shopping district of Oakdale. Wishbone bounded along beside him. Joe's mom had been right—it was going to be a wonderful summer, after all. He had stayed up past his usual bedtime, cramming his head full of information on first editions, trade editions, unauthorized editions, and library bindings. Who'd have thought that books—just books themselves, not even what was in them—could be so interesting?

Joe parked his bike in the alley behind Rosie's Rendezvous Books & Gifts boutique. The back door was locked, so he hurried around to the front. The little bell rang as he came in, and he waved to Mary, who was talking to another clerk behind the counter.

Mary smiled at him. "Hi, Joe. They're waiting for you upstairs."

"*They're* waiting for me?"

Laughing, the other clerk said, "Mr. Gurney's friend is here. Wait till you see them play chess!"

Wondering what she meant, Joe climbed the staircase to the bookstore. He stepped through the doorway and into the thick, dry, dusty smell of old books. Mr. Gurney was right—Joe could imagine that a million rainy afternoons were stored in there. No one was behind the counter. He called out, "Mr. Gurney? Are you here?"

"Back here!" Mr. Gurney's voice floated through the lines of bookshelves. "Just come down Nineteenth-Century Americana to Biographies. Then take a left at Samuel Clemens, a right at Bret Harte, and you'll find us right here at Jack London."

"For heaven's sake, Kilgore," grumbled another voice. "Why not give the boy a ball of string so he can find his way back here after your instructions?"

"No, no, I'm wrong. Take a *right* at Samuel Clemens, a left at Washington Irving, and we're right here at Jack London. Those other directions will take you to the rest rooms!"

Joe followed the sounds of the speakers through the aisles. The two voices got louder as he zigzagged his way toward them.

"Kilgore, you're only confusing the boy."

"Oh, be quiet, Quentin."

Joe came around a glass breakfront filled with elegant leather-bound volumes and stepped into an open space. Armchairs were casually arranged around a table that held a chessboard. Against the wall, the stuffed parrot perched on its stand. Mr. Gurney and another man sat across from each other at the table.

"Hi, Mr. Gurney," Joe said, stepping from an aisle into the reading area.

A smile swept across Mr. Gurney's broad Santa Claus face. "There you are! Joe, meet my good friend, Dr. Quentin Quarrel. Be warned, he lives up to his name!"

The old man at the chessboard stood up from his chair as if his lanky body were hinged together. Where Mr. Gurney was short and round, Dr. Quarrel was tall and lean. Where Mr. Gurney's head was ringed and crowned with snowy white hair, his friend's hair was slicked back and iron-gray, his forehead arching back from a sharp widow's peak. His eyes were a piercing blue and gleamed when he smiled.

"A pleasure to meet you, Mr. Talbot," Dr. Quarrel said, holding out his hand. "Kilgore has been bragging about you all morning. And if I'm quarrelsome, it's only around old fogies who have a lot of bull-headed opinions!" He looked over Joe's shoulder and his smile grew wider. "No wonder he was able to find you in this literary maze, Kilgore. He's using a guide dog!"

"What?" Joe turned, and there, tail wagging happily, sat Wishbone. He looked very satisfied with himself.

"Ah, Wishbone!" Joe sighed as he knelt down and patted his friend on the head. "I thought I left you outside! I'm sorry, Mr. Gurney. He's usually a good dog."

Mr. Gurney said, "Well, maybe before you start work you can take him home—"

Dr. Quarrel threw back his head and then laughed. "Nonsense! It's about time this old place had a proper bookstore dog!"

Wishbone looked as if he were smiling at the tall, elderly man.

Mr. Gurney stroked his white beard. "Well, I don't know . . ."

Dr. Quarrel snorted. "Oh, don't be an old fuddy-duddy, Kilgore! The animal certainly seems well behaved. He'd be a welcome addition to Mr. Faulkner!"

"Mr. Faulkner?" Joe ventured. The *author* William Faulkner? He had been dead for years—or was Dr. Quarrel talking about a literary ghost?

"This is Mr. Faulkner!" Mr. Gurney gestured toward the dusty bird on its perch. "Joe, meet the world's only watch *parrot!*"

Joe gawked at the shadowy shape. "I thought that was . . . I mean, he looks like—"

Dr. Quarrel's sharp voice chuckled behind him. "Thought he was stuffed, didn't you? Common mistake. But, no, he's very much alive—or so Kilgore insists."

Slowly, the dusty green-and-red-feathered head turned and fixed boy and dog with one grumpy eye.

"Cool!" Joe said, stepping closer. "Can he talk?"

"Can, but won't," Dr. Quarrel said. "He picked up the habit of being stubborn from someone right here in this very shop."

"Nonsense!" replied Mr. Gurney. "He speaks when he wants to. Tickle him under the beak. He never bites."

Joe reached out a finger and stroked the bird's throat. The parrot half-closed his eyes and muttered "Thank you" in a squawky voice that made Joe laugh. Wishbone pawed at his friend's leg.

Looking down, Joe said, "What's wrong, boy?"

Wishbone glared up at the parrot that Joe was stroking.

"Someone appears a little jealous," Dr. Quarrel said.

With a final ruffle of the parrot's feathers, Joe said, "It's nice to meet you, Mr. Faulkner." When Joe took his

fingers away, the parrot's head swiveled back around, and its red eye closed.

"There, Kilgore," Dr. Quarrel said. "If you let the dog stay, at least you'll have one guardian awake."

"Well . . . all right," Mr. Gurney answered. "I'll give Wishbone a try. Joe, please remember to walk him at lunchtime."

"Yes, sir."

Mr. Gurney nodded. "Ready to work, Joe? I'm taking Joe into the work area, Quentin. Don't cheat, as you usually do!"

Dr. Quarrel sat back down and made a very elaborate show of studying the chess pieces. He looked up with an expression of outraged innocence. "Kilgore, I am *shocked* that you would even suggest such a thing." He grinned broadly as he dropped Mr. Gurney's white queen into his vest pocket.

Mr. Gurney snorted. "I saw that! Just remember where they were." Then he led Joe to the storage room and clicked on the light.

Joe was interested to see the colorful spines, the part of the book to which the individual pages were attached. "Are all these children's books?" he asked.

"In a way. These four bookshelves in front are the Juvenalia section," Mr. Gurney explained. "However, most of your work will be back here." He led Joe past two tall shelves, mostly empty, to a place where boxes were piled on the floor. From a shelf he took a clipboard that held sheets of paper. "Now, these two are the sorting shelves, where you'll put the books in alphabetical order and check them off this list. After you've done that, then we'll move them to the proper shelves for sale out in the main section of the shop."

Joe took the clipboard and saw that the sheets had

ruled-off spaces to write in author, title, and book condition, and boxes for him to check each off. "I understand."

Mr. Gurney nodded. "You take the books out of the boxes, check them and their conditions off on the list, and then shelve them. Arrange them alphabetically by author. If you find anything unusual, anything that isn't properly described, please make a note."

"I can take care of it, Mr. Gurney." Joe took the clipboard and moved toward the first box. On the side, in careful writing, were the words BOBBSEY TWINS. Mr. Gurney watched his young employee for a moment, then went humming back into the main section of the store. Joe took a book out, checked it off on the list, then set it on the shelf.

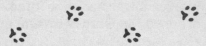

Feeling a little upset about the way Joe had wasted a good scratch on a bird, Wishbone had followed Mr. Gurney and Joe into the storage room. He watched Joe work for a while. Then he stretched. "I think I'll just take a little walk around the place, Joe—sort of discover where everything is. This bookstore dog job can be demanding."

Joe nodded over another book, and Wishbone took that as approval. He hurried back out. The old bookstore was full of interesting smells. Mr. Gurney and Dr. Quarrel seemed engrossed in their chess game. Other people were starting to drift into the store. Someone had begun to brew coffee in the urn next to the cash register, and it added its aroma to the other scents. A dog could get used to this atmosphere!

Wishbone sat on an Oriental rug and watched the customers. Most of them appeared to feel at home, knowing just what they wanted and where to get it. Mr. Gurney

had to leave his chess game now and then to take money for the books.

Wishbone curled up where a friendly sunbeam was making the perfect nap spot in the middle of the rug. Just then he saw a young man wearing a faded-denim shirt and glasses slinking past. *Slinking?* Wishbone perked up. *Yep, I know slinking when I see it, and that guy is definitely slinking! I'd better check this out.*

He followed the bespectacled boy into the History section. The young man looked nervously from side to side. Then he removed a thick book from the shelf. Leaning against the shelf, he began to read.

I guess there's nothing wrong with reading a book in a bookstore, Wishbone thought. *Still, something about him bothers me. Maybe it was the way his footsteps sounded sneaky—just like the ones I heard yesterday. Oh, well, there's lots of other stuff to check out. I'll come back to him later.*

Wishbone rambled through the stacks. A pleasantly plump middle-aged woman in the Romance section absently patted him on the head.

Right. Romance is a nice place to visit for a good pat. Make a note of that.

A rumpled college-professor-type getting a cup of coffee offered Wishbone a stale fig bar, which he munched politely. "Thanks. I suppose it's the thought that counts."

Then Wishbone walked over and checked again on the bespectacled young man. He was still just standing in the aisle, reading the heavy book. His rounds done, Wishbone went back to the rug, curled up on it, and dozed until Joe woke him.

"Come on, boy! Mr. Gurney is giving us an hour for lunch!"

Lunch! What a wonderful word! Wishbone thought. He licked his chops at the very idea of a lunch break. As they passed the History section, Wishbone noticed something odd. The boy was gone, but a young woman with strawberry-blonde hair now stood in his place, reading the very same book! She wore black-rimmed glasses. Wishbone paused. "Hmm . . . That book seems to hold a strange attraction for people. Maybe that's worth keeping an eye on."

"Come *on*, boy!"

Wishbone made a mental note to check back—after lunch and a good nap!

Chapter Three

Still fresh with excitement about his job, Joe called, "Mom! We're home!" A moment later, he and Wishbone burst into the living room.

Ellen came into the room from the kitchen. "Welcome back! I hope that your first full day at work was a good one."

Joe felt proud of himself. "It was great, Mom! Mr. Gurney let me get right to work—unpacking the books, writing down their condition, and shelving them. I've never seen so many books in one place before . . . uh . . . outside of the library, of course."

Ellen laughed. "Well, I'm certainly glad you still think of us poor librarians occasionally."

"Oh, Mom, you know what I meant—but it's like Mr. Gurney said: When you check *his* books out, you get to keep them."

"Come on into the kitchen, you two, and let me hear more about it. Dinner's ready."

Wishbone was suddenly at Joe's side. "I think Wishbone's hungry," Joe said. "Oh—he sort of got a job, too. Mr. Gurney says if he behaves himself, he can be the regular bookstore dog."

"Well, no wonder he's hungry," Ellen said. "Bookstore dogging must be hard work!"

Joe was so excited that he explained all about his job as he helped Ellen set the table. Then he sat down, still talking a mile a minute. "I never knew books like those existed," Joe said, as his mother passed him a bowl of steaming mashed potatoes. "Do you know there's a whole series of books on Zorro? I thought he was just on TV and in the movies. And did I tell you about Tarzan?"

Ellen held up a green bowl. "Yes, you did, dear—take some broccoli, too. It's good for you."

"There are tons of Tarzan books! And there's a whole series about a man named John Carter, who had adventures on Mars with giant green guys with four arms! Mr. Gurney says they're just some of the books kids read before television was invented."

"Kids read them after television came along, too." Ellen leaned back in her chair, a dreamy look on her face.

"I loved this great series about a girl who was a nurse. . . . What was it called? Oh, it's right on the tip of my tongue. . . ." Ellen shook her head. "I can't remember."

"Wishbone was going to have to go home, but Mr. Gurney's friend, Dr. Quarrel, said he was the perfect bookstore dog, and Mr. Gurney agreed. There's a parrot, too, named Mr. Faulkner, and he can talk, and he loves to be scratched under his beak—"

"What's wrong with Wishbone?" Ellen asked abruptly.

Joe looked down. Wishbone lay on the floor, one paw covering his eyes. Feeling puzzled, Joe said, "I don't know, unless he's jealous because I scratched Mr. Faulkner's feathers."

Ellen chuckled.

Wishbone took away his paw and gave them both a disapproving look. Joe laughed. "Well, he *looks* like he's trying to say, 'I'm not jealous of any old bird!'"

Ellen picked up the green bowl and passed it to Joe. "Maybe he's just feeling tired. You still haven't taken any broccoli, Joe."

"Maybe I'll have a little," Joe said.

Wishbone went to his own dish and began to eat, and Joe decided that he was all right. It was strange, though—Wishbone acted as if he resented the parrot. Still, Joe had to admit that Mr. Faulkner added to the fun of his job. He hoped the bird would grow more talkative as it warmed up to him.

As Joe continued to eat his dinner, he couldn't help thinking that, except for the broccoli, it had been an almost perfect day.

33

Wishbone enjoyed the rest of the weekend. On Monday, however, he ran to the store, eager to resume his watchdog duties. Joe was riding his bike to work and had just come around a corner when he slammed on his brakes. The sudden action caused a surprised Wishbone to bump against the rear tire.

"Whoa! Joe, a little warning next time, please!" Wishbone stood staring with his friend at the scene in front of Rosie's.

A police cruiser was parked at the curb out front. A sad-looking Mr. Gurney was talking to a heavyset officer, who nodded and took notes. Joe walked his bike across the street, with a curious Wishbone at his heels.

The policeman, Officer Krulla, turned as they approached. "I'm afraid you can't come any closer, Joe. There's been a break-in."

Joe sounded stunned. "A break-in? Someone broke into Rosie's?"

"No, the bookstore upstairs."

"But I work in the bookstore! This is my boss, Mr. Gurney!"

Mr. Gurney gave Joe a sad smile. "It's all right, Officer Krulla. Joe does work for me—and so does Wishbone." For a few more moments Mr. Gurney talked to the policeman, and then they all went inside Rosie's. They stood at the back of the shop, at the foot of the staircase that led up to Rendezvous Books.

Wishbone immediately began to sniff around. "Boy, talk about sneaky! The crook waited until the faithful bookstore dog was off-duty before he made his move. We're dealing with a professional here, Joe."

"Now, let's take it from the top one more time, Mr. Gurney," said Officer Krulla, putting away his notebook.

"All right. I arrived at the store at eight o'clock.

34

We open at nine, but I like to show up early to start the coffee brewing and straighten up. I let myself in through the alley door behind you there, and I went upstairs. The door to the shop was open, so I knew something was wrong. I'm very careful to shut it every night before I—"

"Yes, sir. And that's when you discovered . . . ?"

"That's when I discovered that during the night some thief had broken into my shop!" Mr. Gurney closed his eyes, as if he were in pain. "The books had been dumped all over the floor. All those beautiful books, just scattered all over the place."

Wishbone was thinking furiously. "How'd he get into the shop?"

Officer Krulla sighed. "Well, it's pretty clear the burglar came in from the alley. A basement window has been smashed." He jerked his thumb over his shoulder, to a closed door marked EMPLOYEES ONLY. "He came up from the basement and into the office of the gift shop, but nothing down here's been disturbed. That's odd. You'd think a burglar would be more interested in some of the stuff down here than in dusty old books."

Mr. Gurney groaned.

Officer Krulla didn't seem to notice. He pointed up the stairway to the bookstore door. "How'd he get that door open up there? That's a pretty solid-looking lock."

"All he had to do was turn the knob," Mr. Gurney said. "In forty years, I've never locked that door."

"Never?" Officer Krulla sounded amazed.

"Never had any need to—before this."

Finally, the officer asked Mr. Gurney to make a list of any missing items. After he left, Joe and Wishbone followed the downcast bookseller toward the staircase. The front door of Rosie's gift shop opened, and Mary Benson came

36

in. "The policeman just told me what happened. Are you all right, Mr. Gurney?" she asked.

"I'll be fine, Mary," he said. "Fortunately, Rosie's seems all right, though I suppose you had better look around to be sure. Rendezvous Books is closed for today. Joe and I are going to have a job on our hands putting it all back together."

Gosh! Wishbone thought as he followed them upstairs. *How bad can it be up there?*

Joe felt his heart sink upon viewing the mess the intruder had made. All the bookshelves in the front of the store stood empty. Books were piled around them like heaps of rocks after an avalanche. Wishbone leaped into action, sniffing around for clues, while Joe and Mr. Gurney started to reshelve the books. They worked silently—Mr. Gurney didn't talk, and Joe couldn't think of anything to say that could even begin to comfort his boss.

"What do you mean, I can't go upstairs!" thundered a voice from downstairs in the gift shop. "I'll have you know, young lady, that I happen to be in the middle of an important chess game that I can't finish because I have the white queen's knight in my trousers pocket! Do you have any idea how difficult it is to play chess without the white queen's knight? . . . What? . . . Go right on up? Well, thank you."

Footsteps rang out on the stairs, and Dr. Quentin Quarrel climbed into view.

"Mary Benson said— What in the world . . . ?" The tall man stood in the doorway, his mouth hanging open, a white chess piece in his right hand.

"We seem to have had a bit of bother, Quentin," said Mr. Gurney with a sigh. "Someone bur——"

"What happened up here—an earthquake? The place is a mess!"

With another heavy sigh, Mr. Gurney told his friend all about the break-in. Dr. Quarrel's piercing blue eyes narrowed.

"This won't do! Send the boy to the storage room to see what's happened to the children's books. I'll help you. What is the world coming to?"

Mr. Gurney told Joe and Wishbone to check the workroom. "And on the way," he added, "make sure Mr. Faulkner is all right. I never even thought to look at him."

Joe stopped at the chess table. The ancient parrot slept peacefully on his perch. Joe changed the newspapers under him on the floor and filled his food and water trays. Then he scratched the parrot's head, prompting a sleepy, muttered "Thank you." Wishbone snorted.

When Joe reached his work area, he saw that the burglar had hit that room, too. Joe set to work, while from the main room he could hear Mr. Gurney and Dr. Quarrel bickering as the two old friends began to put Rendezvous Books back together.

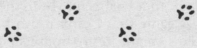

Wishbone stayed out in the stacks, sniffing his way along the rows of shelves. He wanted to see if he could detect anything out of the ordinary, but all he did was sneeze. The burglary had filled the air with book dust—and the dry reek of dusty feathers. *Well,* Wishbone thought as he stared up at Mr. Faulkner's tall perch, *this proves you should never send a bird to do a dog's job!* Maybe people listened when a parrot talked, and maybe Joe might find some weird satisfaction in scratching feathers instead of fur, but it took a dog to be an alert guard. Mr. Faulkner opened one eye and gazed down at Wishbone. It was an irritating kind of glance.

Wishbone returned the stare. "I am *not* going to bark. Nope, not going to do it. I'll explode first!" Just when Wishbone couldn't stand it another moment, the elderly parrot's eye closed again. Wishbone sniffed. "Don't you ever forget that Joe is *my* best friend, you talking feather duster! But right now I have more important things to do—like looking for clues!"

Only there didn't seem to be any. Mr. Gurney and Dr. Quarrel ran back and forth, but very little of the running had anything to do with books. Dr. Quarrel had talked Mr. Gurney into continuing their chess game, so while one of them contemplated the board, the other frantically tried to keep him in sight and shelve books at the same time.

Amazing! Wishbone thought. *Tag Team Shelving.* He didn't know much about chess, but judging from the way the two men played, a large part of the game involved obvious cheating, followed by loud objections.

Then Wishbone's ears perked up at words coming from downstairs: "I've *got* to go upstairs!" A desperate male voice was arguing with Mary down in the gift shop. "Mr. Gurney won't mind. I'm one of his regular customers. Let me just run up and ask him."

Wishbone hurried to the book shop's door. The young man whom he had noticed on Saturday came bounding up the stairs two at a time. Wearing the same denim shirt, he stood in the doorway for a moment and stared around as if he were dazed. "Boy, what a mess!" he said, gasping.

"I'm afraid we're closed for the day," Mr. Gurney said as he came up to him, his arms full of books.

"Did the burglar hit the History section?"

Mr. Gurney blinked at the young man. "I beg your pardon?"

"Whoever broke in didn't mess up History, did he?" The young man seemed frantic, pushing his glasses back up his nose as he talked. Mr. Gurney just stared at him. Finally, the young man took a deep breath and tried to smile. "I—I'm sorry. The clerk downstairs told me about the trouble, and I want to help. I can clean up, or replace books, or anything you need. You know me, don't you, Mr. Gurney?" His smile got more desperate as it became obvious that Mr. Gurney had no idea who he was. "My name's Harold—Harold Whittaker."

Wishbone thought Mr. Gurney still sounded unsure when he murmured, "Oh, yes . . . uh . . . Harold . . . Harold. Well, we could use a little more help—"

"Thank you, sir! I know where the History section is!" Harold was off and running down the aisle before Mr. Gurney could say another word.

This guy is making me more and more curious, Wishbone thought, as he trotted along quietly behind Harold. *I'd better watch him.* Harold actually leaped over piles of books in his race to the History section. When he got there, he frantically began to grab books up off the floor and stuff them onto the shelves.

Wishbone sniffed. "Hey! Hey! Hey! You want to slow down a little? So much for alphabetical order!" Then the young man gasped, pulled one large old book out of the pile, and clasped it to his chest with a contented sigh. Slowly he sank down, his long legs folding up until he was sitting cross-legged on the floor. The book fell open on his lap and, surrounded by stacks of jumbled books, Harold Whittaker began to read.

This is the same section he was in on Saturday, Wishbone thought. *And I'll bet my last doggie ginger snap that's the same book he was reading then. Very peculiar . . .*

Tired and feeling dusty, Joe was just putting a copy of *Tom Corbett, Space Cadet* on the shelf when Mr. Gurney called out, "Time for a break, Joe!"

"Coming, sir!" Joe patted book dust off his shirt. His job was more than half finished. He joined the men in the chess corner. There, Mr. Gurney handed Joe a frosty bottle of soda, and he also introduced him to Harold Whittaker. Dr. Quarrel sat slumped in a chair, sipping his drink with a straw. Joe had no sooner taken his bottle and run the cold glass across his sweating forehead when he heard the distant sound of footsteps approaching from downstairs. It was Mary, and she looked into the shop from the doorway.

"I'm sorry, Mr. Gurney," she began. "I've tried to keep everyone out, but this gentleman insists on—" Then a lean, dark shape appeared behind her, and brilliant teeth flashed.

"Mr. Kilgore Gurney?" The voice that spoke was soft and low, but it still seemed to fill the room the way honey filled a jar.

"Yes, I'm Kilgore Gurney. And you, sir?" he asked as he approached the man.

Joe stared as the dark shape slipped into the bookstore and became a tall, thin young man with black, slicked-back hair and very dark sunglasses. He was wearing a brown shirt and black trousers.

"My name is Jack Brisco." The stranger shook Mr.

Gurney's hand. "I deal in rare books." He glanced around the room. "Miss Benson told me what happened here, and I wanted to offer my sympathy."

"Why, thank you."

Watching them, Joe thought the lean man had the most brilliant white teeth he had ever seen. Brisco's smile was friendly, but the dark glasses that he sported made him look mysterious.

Brisco nodded and said, "I'd like to do a little business." Elegant fingers produced a cream-colored envelope. "I have a long list of demanding customers, and I was hoping you might be able to help me satisfy some of them."

Mr. Gurney took the envelope and removed a sheet of paper. He scanned the list, his eyes grew wide, and he whistled. "My dear sir, I have none of these in my store."

Dr. Quarrel snagged the list, glanced at it, and turned to Mr. Brisco. "Don't pay any attention to Kilgore, Mr.—Brisco, is it? He has no idea what's in this literary graveyard. I'm sure he can come up with just what you're looking for."

"What are you talking about, Quentin?" Mr. Gurney sputtered. "I'd know if I had an autographed first edition of Ray Bradbury's *Dark Carnival!* I'm not a complete idiot, you know!"

"Not complete?" Dr. Quarrel asked with a snort. "Why not? Has some part of you fallen off?"

Joe could not help grinning, and Jack Brisco's smile flashed again. "Just see what you can find, Mr. Gurney. As your friend says, you never really know until you look, right?"

Joe heard a squawk from behind him. It made him jump before he realized it was only Mr. Faulkner. Then Joe winced as the parrot began to speak—or, rather, screech!

42

"Awk! Write what you know! Awk! Write what you know!" The parrot's harsh voice rang out. "Write what you know! Awk! Write what you know!"

Joe felt Wishbone press against his leg. He looked down and saw that Wishbone was staring at Jack Brisco.

As for Mr. Brisco, he merely smiled his gleaming smile. "What an interesting parrot."

"Uh . . . yes," Mr. Gurney said. "He's our unofficial mascot."

"He gives good literary advice. Good day to you, Mr. Gurney." With that final remark, Jack Brisco turned and sauntered out of the shop.

Chapter Four

It took four hours to get the front sections of books reshelved. In Joe's opinion, it would have taken only three if Mr. Gurney and Dr. Quarrel hadn't gotten into an argument over where one of the black knights had been on the board.

Joe could hear them from where he worked his way down the rows of children's books. He'd been embarrassed when the argument started—he felt as if he were eavesdropping. Then he realized that the discussion wasn't really an argument. It wasn't really two grown men yelling angrily at each other. Rather, it was two friends just playing at arguing. *Funny,* Joe thought, *they're just like kids.* He'd laughed to himself at that thought. It was hard to think of the two men as ever having been kids. After that, the sounds of the quarreling had become rather comforting, as Joe had placed book after book on the shelves.

It was warm in the workroom. One long, rectangular skylight cast beams of light across the cluttered bookshelves. Joe wiped sweat off his forehead. He had finished with the Hardy Boys books, and he sat back on the floor to look at them.

The books stood straight and clean across four

shelves, three to six copies of each title. They had been easy to identify and catalogue, because the spines were all numbered. Some were still in tattered dust jackets—those were the more valuable ones—but most were just battered tan volumes. Joe guessed that the original owners had been kids who saved their dimes to buy the books, or who had received them as birthday or Christmas presents.

"Most of these books have kids' names in them," he told Mr. Gurney when the man came in to make sure everything was all right.

"Oh, my word, yes," Mr. Gurney said, caressing a faded blue volume, *The Lone Ranger Returns*. "They belonged to children, and children like to make books their own. And what better way to make a book your own than to put your name in it? For instance, take this one."

Mr. Gurney opened a copy of *The Hardy Boys Number 30: The Wailing Siren Mystery*. On the title page, under the name of the author, Franklin W. Dixon, someone had written: TO A GOOD BOY ON HIS BIRTHDAY. Under that, in a childish scrawl, was: ROGER BLAKE, AGE 10.

"I remember Roger Blake—a little skinny guy with a red crew cut and scabbed knees. They got that way because

he insisted on riding his big brother's old bicycle, and the handlebars came up to his shoulders. He fell off it more than he rode it."

Joe held the book and studied the sprawling signature. He thought it looked faded, and many years old. "What happened to him?"

Mr. Gurney took the book back. "Roger? Oh, he grew up. Went to college. He's a prosperous lawyer in Chicago now, I think."

"Boston!" Dr. Quarrel's voice grumbled from the doorway. "Roger Blake is a journalist in Boston! His brother, Ralph, is a lawyer in Chicago. King's knight to queen's bishop three!"

Shaking his head, Mr. Gurney put the book back on the shelf. "Oh, right, Roger is in Boston, and Ralph is in— What!" He hurried through the doorway. "Your king's knight was nowhere near queen's bishop three!"

Joe shook his head and grinned. Just like kids, he thought again. Roger Blake might be a journalist in Boston, but here among the books of childhood, he would always be a ten-year-old with a red crew cut and skinned knees. *I wonder if he liked books,* Joe thought, *and if he had a dog.* He shivered a little. In this room, Joe had the strange sense of having thousands of Oakdale kids as company—some of them wearing clothes from the fifties. Some were wearing even older clothes from the thirties and forties. It was spooky, Joe thought, but somehow comforting, too, to be part of this timeless world of Oakdale's young people.

Joe had just picked up his clipboard when he heard Mr. Gurney call out, "Lunchtime, Joe! Never let it be said that Kilgore Gurney overworks his employees!"

"He's certainly never overworked himself!" Dr. Quarrel added.

Mr. Gurney roared, "I'll have you know that I'm in excellent shape!"

"You're round, Kilgore."

"*Round* is a shape!"

As Joe opened the workroom door, Wishbone hurried over, tail wagging. "Where have you been, buddy?" Joe rubbed his pal's head. "Taking a nap? Looking for clues about who made this mess? Or just searching for me so you get your share of lunch?"

Wishbone looked indignant, but not so indignant that he didn't grab Joe's pants leg with his teeth and start to pull him toward the chess corner.

"Okay, okay, bad joke, bad joke," Joe said with a laugh. Then he noticed that Wishbone wasn't tugging him toward the others. Instead, he was guiding Joe over to a half-full set of shelves. On the bottom shelf, all by itself, was a book.

Wishbone let go of Joe's jeans leg and sniffed the volume. He yipped and looked around at Joe. Joe picked up the book.

"You're right, boy. This is out of place," he said. The dust jacket, while a bit chipped along the edges, was in generally good shape, and the book inside was obviously well made. Joe read the title. There was something familiar about it.

Mr. Gurney called again. "Lunch is congealing, Joe!"

"Coming!" Joe tucked the strange book under his arm and hurried through the aisles, with Wishbone right behind him.

The smell of pepperoni made Joe's mouth water. The chess game had been carefully removed from the table and set down on the floor. In its place was a gigantic flat cardboard box with its lid open. Big red letters on the lid spelled out PEPPER PETE'S PIZZA.

Mr. Gurney sat in his chess chair, leaning over the lid of the box to keep the golden cheese from dribbling all over his trousers. Dr. Quarrel had a napkin the size of a sheet tucked into his collar and was nibbling away with his eyes closed. Harold Whittaker stood to one side with a slice in each hand, eating as if he were afraid someone was going to take them away from him. As soon as Joe saw what was in the box, he understood.

"A Pepper Pete's Super-Extra-Large Triple Pepperoni Special!" He breathed in the delicious, spicy aroma. "Wow! Even Sam and David and I have never ordered a Super-Extra-Large!"

"Nothing's too good for my employees." Mr. Gurney laughed expansively. "Paid assistant or volunteer, everyone feasts!"

"Get yourself a slice, Joe," Dr. Quarrel snapped. "Reduce the number available for your employer. Too much cholesterol is bad for certain body types."

Mr. Gurney paused in mid-bite. "Quentin, anyone would think you were a doctor of medicine instead of philosophy!"

With a grunt, Dr. Quarrel snapped, "You don't need a glass eye to tell if a goldfish is marble or wood."

Mr. Gurney looked at his friend in astonishment. "That didn't make any sense at all!"

"It's philosophy," growled Dr. Quarrel. He munched a bite of pizza, swallowed, then added, "Philosophy doesn't have to make sense. In fact, it's often more respected if it doesn't!"

Joe grinned, nodded to Harold—who nodded back but didn't miss a bite—and held out the unfamiliar book. "Wishbone found something."

The tall old man said, "Reading on the job? Careful, Joe, down that road lies bookstore ownership."

"I wasn't really reading," said Joe, helping himself to a dripping slice of pizza. "We found this on a nonfiction shelf toward the back."

"Isn't that always the way?" Mr. Gurney sighed heavily, dabbing his lips with a paper napkin. "People decide they want a book, carry it halfway through the store, change their mind, and put it down anywhere. . . ." His voice trailed off as he stared blankly at the black book.

Dr. Quarrel glared at him. "What's the matter, Kilgore? Pepperoni got your tongue?"

"It's *Dark Carnival,*" Mr. Gurney said almost breathlessly, wiping his fingers with a napkin before reverently picking up the book.

Dr. Quarrel asked, "What about it?"

In a shaky voice, Mr. Gurney said, "This is a copy of Ray Bradbury's *Dark Carnival!* Is it a first edition? Of course it's a first—it only came in a first!"

Dr. Quarrel reached for another slice of pizza. "Sounds familiar. Wasn't the young man in the dark glasses looking for that?"

"But I don't have a copy of *Dark Carnival!* I'd know if I did. Look at the dust jacket—its condition is at least Fine, maybe even Extra-Fine!"

Joe looked up from where he was putting a slice of pizza on an old newspaper for Wishbone. "Is it hard to find in that condition?"

Harold Whittaker had craned his neck to see the book. "This is Ray Bradbury's first book, printed by a specialty press called Arkham House. It's probably worth a bundle."

Mr. Gurney feverishly turned the pages. "Just a tad foxed, barely noticeable." He glanced at the title page and gasped.

Wondering about Mr. Gurney's startled expression, Joe asked, "What's wrong?"

Blinking, Mr. Gurney muttered, "Wrong? Nothing's wrong. This is so— It's inscribed!"

He held the book up, and Joe could see BEST! FROM RAY BRADBURY, written in spiky, angular handwriting.

Dr. Quarrel let out a whistle. "Autographed! My stars, Kilgore!"

"Where is that list Mr. Brisco left? I have to call him!" Mr. Gurney dashed to the sales counter and started tossing bits of paper all over the place.

Joe turned to Dr. Quarrel, who was shaking his head and looking as if he were trying not to laugh. "Dr. Quarrel, that book wasn't on the store's inventory list."

"I'm sure it wasn't, Joe. Kilgore would keep it under lock and key. Don't let it surprise you—Kilgore isn't noted for his great record keeping!"

"I found it!" Mr. Gurney called, waving the cream-colored paper over his head as he started dialing his old rotary phone.

"Good for you! Hurry so I can get back to beating you at chess!" Dr. Quarrel replied. He smiled. "Well, this is good luck for Kilgore. He always buys more books than he can sell. A volume like this is a real find for him. He may have hired you just in time, Joe. Keep a sharp eye out. There's no telling what else may be squirreled away in here."

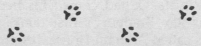

Wishbone stared at Mr. Faulkner. The parrot was awake, but he was gazing at the door, not at Wishbone. Wishbone cocked his head. "Come on, bird. You know something. That's as plain as the beak on your face . . .

well, maybe not that plain. Anyway, you must have seen whoever broke in here. You can tell me. I'm the Official Bookstore Dog."

Unfortunately, Mr. Faulkner paid no attention to the Official Bookstore Dog. He just kept staring at the landing, his unfriendly red eyes never blinking.

Wishbone ate a final bit of pizza crust as he thought about the break-in. Mr. Gurney hung up the phone, went to the door, and called down to Mary to say that the bookstore was open again. Within a few minutes, customers began to come up the staircase. Wishbone recognized many of them. The plump lady came in and disappeared into the Romance section. The college professor also returned, nodded pleasantly to Dr. Quarrel, and settled into one of the armchairs with an old mystery novel and a bag of fig bars. Wishbone wrinkled his nose. How could humans eat those things—and not offer one to the noble dog?

For the rest of the afternoon, Wishbone followed Harold around—as much as he could follow a person who didn't move much. Harold had anchored himself in the History section for more than an hour, reading from his mysterious book. Finally the young man sighed, nodded, and put the big book back in its proper place. He went down the aisle, and Wishbone heard him thank Mr. Gurney for the pizza.

Wishbone scratched his chin thoughtfully. Why did Harold seem so suspicious? Well, he seemed to know a lot about the Bradbury book, for one thing. Then, too, there was the furtive way he read that big, fat volume, nervously glancing around as if he were afraid of being caught doing something. Wishbone lay down at the foot of one of the old chairs and put his head on his paws.

A shadow fell across him, and Wishbone sat bolt upright. A young woman had slipped into the store, nervously adjusting her black-rimmed glasses. She had pale strawberry-blond hair and was dressed in jeans and a T-shirt, just as she had been on Saturday. Wishbone watched her suspiciously. She walked down an aisle, and Wishbone followed.

Straight to the History section.

The young woman looked both ways, then reached up for the exact same book Harold had been reading. Carefully, she placed it on an empty shelf, opened it, and began to read.

Wishbone settled down to watch her. He was beginning to think that Rendezvous Books had been attacked by a pack.

Maybe, he thought, he already knew two of the members.

The bookstore dog decided he had work to do.

Chapter Five

Just before closing time, a weary Joe was replacing his clipboard on its shelf behind the sales counter when Mr. Gurney came over holding a battered black book. "I kept thinking I had seen this someplace," Mr. Gurney said, smiling down at the volume. "I have three copies of this, and this one's far from the best. For some reason I didn't discard it. Maybe I was waiting for you to show up. Here, Joe. I want you to have this. Call it a bonus for finding that copy of *Dark Carnival*."

Wondering what in the world the book could be, Joe took it from his boss. He could see right away that it certainly wasn't an Extra-Fine, or even a Fine. In book-seller's terms, it was only a Reading Copy, battered and shabby, with a split spine. Joe opened it and saw that the pages were foxed and dusty. "Uh . . . thanks, Mr. Gurney," Joe said, puzzled at this odd gift.

"Look at the title page, Joe," Mr. Gurney told him. "Then you may understand why I want to give this book to you."

Joe carefully turned the brittle pages. Then he stood blinking, feeling happy and sad all at the same time. The book was called *The Haunted Bookshop,* and it was by Christopher Morley. That didn't mean anything to Joe.

For him, the wonderful part was what was written in pencil on the blank page opposite the title page:

This book belongs to
Stevie Talbot—
Grade 6.

The blocky, printed letters had faded to a light gray. Joe touched them, hardly breathing.

"Did I guess right?" asked Mr. Gurney in a gentle voice.

Joe nodded and swallowed the lump in his throat. "Steve Talbot was my dad. Thank you, Mr. Gurney."

Mr. Gurney patted him on the shoulder. "I knew your name sounded familiar. I just didn't make the connection until the burglar broke in. There's a peculiar bookstore burglar in that book, too, you see, and— But I don't want to keep you, or to spoil the story. You can read it all for yourself."

Wishbone waited at the door. Downstairs, out in the alleyway, Joe climbed on his bike and they started for home. As he pedaled, Joe kept thinking of his father. Steve Talbot had been a basketball coach at Oakdale College. When Joe was only six years old, his father had died of a rare blood disorder. Now Joe had a book that his father had actually owned as a kid. It made him feel a strange sort of connection with the past.

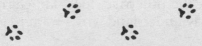

At home, Joe showed Ellen the book. She looked at it carefully, her eyes bright. "Your father always loved mysteries," she said softly. "Take good care of it, Joe."

"I will," Joe assured her. After dinner, he took the

volume straight up to his room and kicked off his shoes. Sitting propped up in bed with Wishbone curled up at his side, Joe began to read the book.

The story was about a New York bookshop and an ordinary sort of book that someone stole from it. Joe could understand why the burglary at Rendezvous Books had jogged Mr. Gurney's memory of *The Haunted Bookshop*. After finishing the first chapter, Joe turned back to the page where his dad had written his name.

Joe shivered, feeling once again that strange sense of being among a whole ghostly crowd of Oakdale's young people, past and present. He touched the faded letters and smiled. "I never thought of my dad as a kid, not a real kid like me or Sam or David. It's kind of . . . neat, you know, Wishbone?"

Wishbone made a little sighing noise that sounded a lot like agreement.

From downstairs came the faint sound of the front doorbell, interrupting Joe's thoughts. He hopped up and reached for his sneakers. "That'll be Sam and David. Come on, boy," Joe said. After laying the book on his bureau, he led Wishbone back downstairs.

Joe was happy to see his friends, who were full of excitement over their own jobs. David was getting to show off his skill with computers. Sam was not only working inside Pepper Pete's, but she was occasionally getting to make deliveries on a moped!

"Cool!" Joe said. And then he told them about lunch at the book shop.

"A Super-Extra-Large Triple Pepperoni Special?" David asked, his eyes bright at the very idea.

"Joe's right," Sam confirmed. "I delivered it myself. It was a special trip—I could barely fit that box so that it would stay on the moped!"

"We had that once," David said, smiling at the memory. "My dad bought it to celebrate when I aced math. We still had slices left over for breakfast the next day."

Joe couldn't help laughing. "Pizza for breakfast? What a concept!" He turned and called into the kitchen, "Hey, Mom! Can we have pizza for—"

"Ask me after Sam's dad comes up with a bacon-and-scrambled-egg pizza," Ellen called back.

With mischief in his heart, Joe teased, "How about it, Sam?"

She gave him a long look. "I don't know—it could be interesting."

David said, "Bacon, scrambled eggs, and pepperoni. Hold the anchovies."

The three friends laughed their heads off. Wishbone glanced up from his big red chair, yawned, then promptly went to sleep.

Joe told his friends about the break-in and all the trouble it had caused.

"Did you get all the books put back?" Sam asked, twirling her baseball cap on one finger.

Joe sighed, remembering the chaos. "Finally. Books were scattered all over the floor. It was a real mess—sort of."

"Sort of?" David frowned. "What does that mean?"

Shaking his head and thinking it over, Joe replied, "That's the *really* strange thing about all this. You'd think a burglar wouldn't be . . . well . . . neat—" Ellen came in and placed a bowl of popcorn on the coffee table, and Joe said, "Thanks, Mom."

"Wait a minute," Sam said, taking a big fistful of popcorn. "I never heard of a neat burglar. What did he steal?"

Joe shrugged. "We don't know what he took yet. Still, if someone was going through looking for specific books, you'd think he would have thrown the ones he didn't want down any old way instead of stacking them neatly."

David said, "Lucky for you that he didn't."

Joe had to agree. "Now we have to figure out what he took," he said. "So far, Mr. Gurney hasn't come up with anything that seems to be missing."

"Maybe it isn't something obvious," Sam pointed out. "It could be something small."

Joe nodded, thinking this over. That was possible.

In his big red chair, Wishbone opened his eyes and raised his head. Joe thought that Wishbone, too, looked as if he were puzzled by the strange break-in.

Feeling much fresher, a rested Joe was at the store early the next morning, but Officer Krulla had arrived before him. Joe found the stocky policeman standing beside the cash register, talking to Mr. Gurney.

"*Nothing* was stolen?" Officer Krulla asked, scratching his thinning brown hair and looking bewildered.

"Nothing that we can tell so far." Mr. Gurney sighed. "Hello, Joe. We're still doing the inventory, so we're not absolutely sure."

Wishbone trotted past the policeman and vanished between two bookshelves.

Officer Krulla looked from Mr. Gurney to Joe, then back again. "I think that will be all for now, Mr. Gurney. If anything else comes up, or if you discover something really is missing, give us a call. Otherwise, we'll be in touch." The police officer left the store.

Joe wondered what the police might do now. "Is Officer Krulla going to help you find the burglar?" he asked.

Mr. Gurney shrugged. "Unfortunately, that will be hard to do. I think we just have to hope that we won't be visited again."

A rumbling laugh from the chess corner told Joe that Dr. Quarrel was already there. He looked down the aisle and waved at the tall man, who winked at him as he switched a black rook for a white bishop. In his loud voice, Dr. Quarrel called, "Why didn't you tell Officer Krulla the rest of it, Kilgore?"

Mr. Gurney began to stock the cash register with bills and coins from a bank pouch. "I have no idea what you're talking about, Quentin."

Dr. Quarrel reached out and tapped one long finger on the small stack of books next to the chess board. "Ah, yes, I understand. It might be embarrassing explaining to one of Oakdale's finest how a break-in could be the best thing that ever happened to Rendezvous Books. It showed you books you didn't know you had."

"We would have found them anyway," Mr. Gurney mumbled into his chest.

Wishbone had wandered up and down the aisles. Now he came back and sat beside Joe's feet. Joe picked up his clipboard and left the two men as they continued to argue. Wishbone padded along with him. The two went into the sorting room. Joe opened a box and stared at what should have been a stack of *Oz* books by L. Frank Baum and Ruth Plumly Thompson.

Wishbone braced his front legs on the edge of the box and took deep sniffs of the top book. He yipped and looked up at Joe as if he expected Joe to do something. Joe could tell that the top book did not belong among *Wizard of Oz* stories. He picked it up and, with his heart beating fast, he opened it. Then he hurried back to the front counter.

"Wishbone and I found another one, Mr. Gurney," Joe said, holding the volume out.

The elderly man slumped over, leaned his white head against the cash register, and sighed. "What is it this time, Joe?"

Joe felt sorry for his boss. "*The Little Sister.* A mystery by Raymond Chandler, sir. It was in a box of *Oz* books. Wishbone seemed to know it was out of place. Maybe it smells different to him."

Mr. Gurney's head shot up. "Raymond Chandler?" He took the book and murmured, "Very nice. The dust jacket has a tear down the back, but it's been lovingly taped. Sound binding. Good condition." He opened the book. "And the autograph has been tipped in."

"Tipped in?" Joe asked. "What does that mean?"

Mr. Gurney held the book so that Joe could see the title page and put his finger on the signed name. "It means the book itself isn't actually signed. The original owner may have written a fan letter to Mr. Chandler, who probably wrote a short note back. The owner then cut out the signature and pasted it here facing the title page. He *tipped in* the signature."

Joe was uncertain of what that might mean. "Is that a good thing?"

"Raymond Chandler created the private eye Philip Marlowe, Joe," Mr. Gurney said, carefully leafing through the book. "Many people equate him with Sherlock Holmes as far as fictional detectives go. Yes, this is a good thing, a valuable book to a collector." Peering down over the rims of his glasses, Mr. Gurney solemnly said, "Thank you, Wishbone." The Jack Russell terrier seemed to grin back up at him. Mr. Gurney looked back at the book and carefully turned another page, a worried smile on his face. "How could I have possibly misplaced this?"

"What did you find now?" Dr. Quarrel shouted. "Hurry up and lose this game, won't you?"

Mr. Gurney placed the book on the counter. "Joe found a first edition of *The Little Sister*," he called back. "Dust jacket slightly damaged, autograph tipped in. Someone would pay a lot for this item. I wish I knew where it came from."

"Your mother probably bought it forty years ago, Kilgore." Dr. Quarrel snorted, coming over to the counter. He picked up the book. "It wasn't all that valuable then. It got put in the wrong box, left on the wrong shelf—be glad you've got it now."

"Yes, yes, you're right, of course." said Mr. Gurney. "I'll just take it and the Bradbury and put them in the Rare and Collectible cabinet for Mr. Brisco. I'd hate to misplace them again."

"Keep your eyes peeled on the way," Dr. Quarrel called after him. "No telling what you might find between here and there!"

Mr. Gurney laughed softly. He gathered up the

books and walked off into the stacks. "And don't think I haven't noticed there are *three* black bishops on the board!" he said over his shoulder.

Joe wondered why Mr. Gurney seemed so subdued—sad, almost. He asked, "Shouldn't Mr. Gurney be happier about finding these valuable books, Dr. Quarrel?"

Dr. Quarrel leaned on the counter. "One would think so, Joe. These finds mean money for him. I must say, Kilgore's got the luck of the Irish."

Sometimes Joe found Dr. Quarrel's way of expressing himself difficult to follow. He asked, "You mean if it hadn't been for the break-in, Mr. Gurney might never have found those books?"

With a wink, Dr. Quarrel replied, "That's a possibility. There's been a bookstore up here since the forties, and it's always been run by one Gurney or another." Dr. Quarrel laughed, his blue eyes sparkling. "Gurneys are absent-minded folk. Yes, this break-in could just be the best thing ever to happen to Kilgore."

Joe returned to work. He still felt in his bones that something very strange indeed was going on at Rendezvous Books. He heard the two men resume their chess game. Every now and then, Dr. Quarrel's hearty laugh came ringing sharp and clear. Joe wondered what the joke was this time—Mr. Gurney's absent-mindedness, the break-in that had led to the discovery of rare books, or just more creative chess cheating.

While Joe worked, Wishbone made his Official Bookstore Dog rounds. Supremely watchful, he trotted up and down the aisles, patrolling with pride.

Right, Gardening is okay. Right, everything is fine in

Poetry. Nothing is going on in Drama. Wishbone glanced alertly from side to side, checking out the books and their readers and thinking.

American Literature, check. English Literature, double check. His tail whipped back and forth. *Everything's fine with the books, but something very odd is going on here. I can smell it as clearly as an old Pepper Pete's take-out box on a hot day!*

Wishbone gnawed on the problem as if it were a juicy bone. He paused in Mystery. A few displaced books were still stacked on the floor, waiting for Mr. Gurney or Dr. Quarrel to take time from their eternal chess games and arguments to shelve them. Wishbone sniffed at the first stack, sneezing as book dust flew up his nose.

A-choo! He shook his head to clear it. "This isn't a clue, it's an allergy attack waiting to happen." After sneezing again, Wishbone turned around several times and settled down next to the books, realizing something. The volumes had all been lying on the floor as if they had been stacked there and then carefully knocked over. "Now, *that's* the problem," Wishbone told himself. "Why would a burglar *carefully* take a row of books off their shelf, *carefully* stack them on the floor, and then *carefully* knock them over? That's not burglary or vandalism, that's redecorating! Clues that don't make any sense aren't really clues at all."

Eventually, as Wishbone began to drift into a nap, something nagged at his memory. He had that strange sense called *déjà vu*, the impression that all of this had happened before.

Yes, he thought, *something strange is going to happen. I feel that in my bones. Oh, I'd give my favorite chew toy to learn exactly what it might be!*

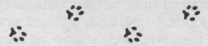

Another Friday morning came. Wishbone raced behind Joe's bicycle, and his mind raced ahead of them both. *Think, think, think! Let's get that fine doggie mind going! Gotta get a handle on this! It's probably so simple a cat could figure it out! Brrr! There's a nasty thought!* Then they were inside Rosie's Rendezvous and running upstairs to the bookstore.

Again Wishbone patrolled the aisles. Joe worked in Juvenalia. Mr. Gurney and Dr. Quarrel played something that seemed like chess. Wishbone trotted around the corner of History, and there stood Harold Whittaker, engrossed in the same book that Wishbone had seen him with before. Was Harold part of the oddness Wishbone sensed? Hmm . . . He came to the shop almost every day, went to the same spot, and had done far less picking up than anyone else after the break-in. Then, too, Harold certainly *looked* guilty. He kept glancing around, but he never seemed to notice Wishbone's steady gaze.

Finally, Harold checked his watch and put the book back on the shelf, slowly, reluctantly. Then, with a sigh, he stuffed his hands in his pockets and shuffled toward the door. He looked left and right, as if fearing someone was following him.

Wishbone's eyes narrowed. "Aha! Suspicious Harold is on the move!" He decided he could leave the bookstore in human hands for a while.

Wishbone set out to follow Harold Whittaker. The alert terrier padded silently downstairs, through Rosie's, and up to the front door. Mary noticed him and let him out. Wishbone's nose told him to turn left, and soon he had Harold in sight.

Harold walked slowly down Main Street, his hands still in his pockets, his shoulders hunched forward into the summer heat. Wishbone shadowed him from half a block behind.

"If he glances back, I'll just pretend to be window-shopping. . . . Hmm . . . Beck's Grocery smells as if it has some great steaks in the meat department. No, stay on the job, Wishbone. Investigate!"

Harold ambled on. At the corner, the young man crossed the street and then turned left. He paused outside Pepper Pete's. Wishbone also stopped and took another deep sniff.

"Okay, we've got cheese, pepperoni, Italian sausage, hamburger—makes me hungry."

Harold stared wistfully at the menu in the window. Wishbone could see a crowd of people inside. There was Sam, carrying a pizza to a family sitting near the door.

Harold tore himself away from Pepper Pete's window. Reluctantly, Wishbone left the delicious aromas behind to follow him. They passed the Royal Theater and the high school. Wishbone realized they were heading for Oakdale College. That made sense—Harold had the lean and hungry look of a college freshman!

Just before Harold reached the campus, he turned to the right. There, tucked between two old oaks, was a hot-dog wagon. A young man stood behind it. He glanced up as Harold approached and smiled. "'Lo, Harold—the usual?"

"'Lo, Marty." Harold sighed deeply. "The usual."

Marty reached for a bun. "Sure I can't interest you in a foot-long? Only fifty cents more."

Harold laughed ruefully. "No, thanks. Buying supplies for the summer term just about wiped me out. I have to stretch my food budget until I get paid."

"Okay, that's one regular with mustard and catsup, a sprinkle of onions, no sauerkraut, and a root beer."

Harold counted out coins while the hot-dog man expertly jabbed a wiener and popped it into a bun. In a jiffy the hot dog was ready, covered with mustard and catsup and just a little bit of onion. Harold handed over his coins, took the hot dog, and walked onto the campus. He sat on a marble bench under an oak tree and began to eat his lunch.

Wishbone licked his chops. "Well, there won't be any leftovers for the noble dog, that's for sure!" From behind a tree, the Jack Russell terrier watched until Harold had finished eating, tossed the waxed paper and paper cup into a trash can, and headed on across campus.

Deciding it was time to return to his bookstore duties, Wishbone walked away in deep thought. *Okay, now I know that Harold has very little money, so he might want to steal books. Yet, if he were the thief, he probably wouldn't show up at the shop every day—unless he does it to throw off suspicion. Oh, catburgers!*

By the time he got back to Rosie's, Wishbone felt thoroughly confused. "Okay," he told himself, "maybe the thing to do is to check out that book Harold is always reading. I wonder if it smells like those special books Joe and I have found. I know one way to find out!" He scratched politely at the front door, and Mary let him back inside.

Upstairs, Wishbone paced with authority through the stacks. Yes, everything had held together while he had been out. The Romance lady stopped her browsing long enough to scratch his ears, and the professor had absently tossed him a fig bar—which he ate.

"Mmm . . . not as good as a pizza or even a hot dog, but beggars can't be choosers. I should know. I'm tops at begging!"

Wishbone stopped by the storage and sorting room long enough to check up on Joe. *Oh, good,* Wishbone thought. *This time Mr. Gurney has sent out for hamburgers, and Joe has saved me some.*

Then he went over to the History section. High up over his head was the leather-bound volume that Harold had paid so much attention to. "Hmm . . . perhaps a little careful jumping is in order here."

Wishbone wiggled down, laid his sights on the book, then leaped high up into the air. His head shot out and his nose bumped into the book's spine. *Oww! That hurts! Well, faint heart never won fair squeak toy!* Then he hunkered down and leaped again and again.

Oww! Oww! Oww! If only I could get one good sniff!

Just when it seemed that the heavy book would surely fall and Wishbone would at last unlock its secrets, a slim arm shot out and rescued it. Wishbone looked up in exasperation. "Hey, get your own book! Whoa! I guess it *is* your book!"

The slim arm belonged to Harold's counterpart, the bespectacled young woman with whom he shared the mysterious book every day. She clutched it to her T-shirt and breathed a sigh of relief.

Sitting, Wishbone stared up at her. "That must be some book you have there, lady. What is it? *Great Burglaries of History? Thefts of the Century? My Life in Crime?*"

The young woman smiled down at Wishbone. She pushed her glasses back up her nose as she did so. Then, in a very unsuspicious move, she knelt down and scratched his head.

"You look like a really smart dog, but I don't think even a smart dog would be interested in Gibbon's *Decline and Fall of the Roman Empire.*"

Chapter Six

J oe walked into Pepper Pete's and craned his head to look around. He saw Sam and David at a table in the back. They waved, and Joe and Wishbone hurried over.

It was Saturday afternoon, and Pepper Pete's was crowded with regulars. There were students from Oakdale College among them, as well as a noisy bunch of kids celebrating a T-ball victory. Joe had the afternoon off. Sam had invited him over to share an on-the-house pizza with her and David.

Joe was soon digging into a delicious slice. At his feet, Wishbone happily munched his, neatly placed on a paper plate.

David asked, "Say, did they ever find out anything more about the break-in over at the bookstore?"

Between bites, Joe filled his friends in on the latest news from the Great Bookstore Break-In—which wasn't very much.

"No clues at all?" David said. "Boy, that's odd."

Joe sighed happily as he finished his slice of pizza. "I know, but as I said, everything was just kind of messed up. Even that was strange. The books were all over the floor, but in alphabetical order right next to the shelves they're supposed to be on. Most of the time I didn't even have to check them. I just picked them up and put them back on the shelves."

Sam said thoughtfully, "Maybe that shows you're up against really professional burglars who know exactly what they're looking for."

"Maybe," Joe agreed. "Another odd thing is that we keep finding valuable books that aren't on the store's inventory list."

David nodded. "How many have you guys found?"

Deciding against attempting another slice, Joe replied, "Five, as of yesterday. None of them is in the right place. Some were on the wrong shelves, some in boxes. Dr. Quarrel says they've probably been there for years, and if it hadn't been for the burglary, they might have been misplaced forever."

David picked up another slice and bit into it thoughtfully. "Someone breaks in, and *then* you begin to find books you didn't know you had? Bizarre!"

Joe nodded. "I'm starting to read a book that's kind of like what's happening at the book shop. It's a mystery that takes place in a bookstore called Parnassus, and what is strange is that burglars steal just one book from it."

"A mystery!" Sam said, looking up from her pizza. "And the police haven't returned?"

With a shrug, Joe said, "Officer Krulla came in once for a list of stolen books, but we haven't found anything missing yet. He hasn't come back since then."

David raised his eyebrows. "He didn't even bother to investigate?"

"Well . . . no," Joe replied. "It isn't a robbery if nothing if stolen. I don't know if breaking and stacking is a real crime—is it?"

Sam pushed away her plate with its half-eaten slice of pizza. Her eyes were dancing as she said, "Breaking and *entering* is a real crime! If the police aren't looking for clues, maybe we can."

Joe grinned. "That's exactly what I was thinking!" He dropped his crusts on Wishbone's plate, and Wishbone happily polished them off.

Sam was practically bouncing in her chair. "This is *our* chance to do some detective work. We just need to go look, that's all. Come on, guys, it'll be fun, and it just might help."

David's expression showed he was not convinced. "Guys, we shouldn't go messing in police business."

Joe couldn't help smiling. David could be almost overly cautious sometimes, except when it came to his science projects. "Come on—Officer Krulla didn't say we *couldn't* look for clues. We can't get into the store right now, though. Mr. Gurney closes early on Saturday so he and Dr. Quarrel can go to the Oakdale Chess Club meeting at the college."

Sam folded her arms over her chest until Joe fell silent. "You got my hopes up for nothing."

"I'm not going to sneak into the store," Joe said. "That wouldn't be right." He got up, grinning. "But if you guys want to come with me, we'll take a look in the alley behind it!"

Soon the three friends were pedaling down Main Street to Rendezvous Books. A thoughtful Joe pumped along in front, with Sam and David following closely. Wishbone charged along with them, running happily through the warmth of the late afternoon. The sun was about to set when they pulled up in front of Rosie's Rendezvous and parked their bikes.

"I don't know, Joe," David said, looking up at the cloudy sky. "It's starting to get pretty dark. And it looks like rain."

With Wishbone trotting a few steps ahead, Joe strode back toward the alley. Without looking around, he said, "Then we have to get started right away and not waste any time."

Sam said, "Come on, David." Hurrying to catch up to Joe, she continued, "Okay, so he didn't come in through the front door. Then, how did he get in?"

Joe reached the alley and looked back. "Officer Krulla says the burglar came in the back way." He pointed, and Sam and David stared off behind the store. There, tucked away between Rosie's and the building behind it, was a narrow little alley. Wishbone was already sniffing around the area.

David sounded unsure when he said, "It looks pretty . . . dark."

Joe had to agree. With the clouds growing thicker, afternoon had become a gloomy dusk. The alley's mouth was as dark as a cave opening. The kids looked at it for a long time. In the distance, thunder rumbled.

"It does sort of look creepy," Sam said. She tried to see down the alley without actually entering it.

Wishbone, who had come back to them, suddenly pricked up his ears and ran into the dark space, giving one excited bark.

"Well, it can't be *too* bad," Joe said. "Wishbone went in alone."

Together, the three followed Wishbone into the alley. Joe shivered. He knew perfectly well that the squat shapes against the walls were just trash cans, but in the gloom they looked ominous. A gust of wind swept a newspaper down the alley. Wishbone chased it, but the wind lifted

the flapping paper. It dashed at Joe's face and then soared overhead, like a ghost escaping from a tomb.

"I'm with Sam," David whispered. "It seems creepy to me."

"Maybe it wouldn't be if someone ever emptied these garbage cans and took away the trash stacked on top," Sam whispered back.

"They empty the cans twice a week, just like every place else in town," Joe said, feeling obligated to defend Mr. Gurney's alley. "The garbage is going to be picked up on Monday. And why are you guys whispering?"

"I always whisper in alleys," Sam said defensively. "You're supposed to whisper in alleys—I thought everyone knew that."

Thunder growled again, nearer this time, and a cool breeze drifted through the darkness. The storm was getting closer. Up ahead, Wishbone stood by an old door, filling the narrow space with excited barking.

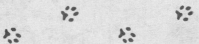

"Will you guys hurry?" Wishbone barked again. "You'd think you'd never been in a scary old alley before! Come on, come on, we've got mysteries to solve!"

Joe stopped to pat his friend on the head before he turned to the others. "This is the back door to the bookstore—well, it's the back door to Rosie's, but Mr. Gurney uses it so he doesn't have to haul his books through the front door."

"It looks pretty ordinary to me," David said, peering intently at it. It was an old metal delivery door set flush with the brick wall. There was a small window in it that someone had painted over long ago, and a battered light fixture hung just overhead.

"It's ordinary, all right," Sam said in a disgusted voice. "It smells like garbage, and I don't see any clues."

Wishbone couldn't believe his ears. "What! You're not looking, Sam! There are fat, juicy clues all over the place, right under your nose! Or there would be, if humans had real noses. . . . Oh, what's the use? No one ever listens to the dog."

"Um . . . just what kind of clues are we looking for?" David asked, as a fat raindrop plopped down in front of him.

"Anything unusual," Joe said. "It's starting to rain. Maybe we'd better look fast."

Raindrops pattered down, making a sound like running mice. Wishbone leaped up and down in front of the door. "Look up, guys! Come on, look up!"

Joe knelt next to Wishbone. "What's the matter, boy? You trying to tell us something?" he asked, concern in his voice.

Wishbone stared at his friend. "Oh, come on, Joe! Look up!"

Finally, Joe glanced up, still petting Wishbone. "Guys! I think Wishbone found a clue!"

Wishbone proudly licked Joe's hand. "That's my buddy Joe! He *can* be taught!"

Sam and David huddled around Joe and Wishbone and looked up into the drizzling sky. Sam said, "I see the windows up there, with no lights in them."

"You're getting warm," Joe said, "but that's not the clue I meant."

"Joe, what are you talking about?" David asked. "Where? Show me."

Joe stood and pointed. "Someone's broken the light bulb in the fixture over the back door. Look at the glass on the ground."

73

"That's a clue?" David frowned.

"It's the only light fixture in this whole alley, so it'd be the only light, period. The burglar—or whatever he was—must have smashed the bulb so no one would see him break in."

"That's good thinking," Sam said. "We're on the right track."

Suddenly, the thunder boomed right overhead and the sky opened up, pouring rain into the alley—and drenching them all.

"Run!" Joe yelled.

"But all the clues will be washed away!" Sam wailed, stuffing her prized delivery hat under her Pepper Pete's jacket. The kids pounded back up the alley through a solid wall of water, leaped on their bikes, and sped off, wincing at the cold rain.

Wishbone ran alongside them, his sharp canine mind going a mile a minute. *Not all the clues, Sam. Not by a long shot. If you humans had ears as good as mine, you could have heard the other clue. I sure did. Even through that old closed door and a whole floor away, I heard it.*

It was the harsh voice of Mr. Faulkner screeching at the top of his rusty old parrot lungs, "Write what you know! Awk! Write what you know!"

Chapter Seven

Wishbone felt cold, soaked, and miserable. He gave himself a good long shake. "Wet, wet, wet! Yuck, yuck, yuck!"

Joe gasped, "Stop shaking, Wishbone!"

Outside, sheets of rain lashed against the side of the Talbots' house. Joe knelt in front of the fireplace, a thick towel in his hands. He had brought it to dry Wishbone, but now he held it in front of him as a shield. His mother stood behind him and laughed.

Wishbone gave Joe an apologetic look. "Sorry, Joe. I can't fight my doggie instincts!"

Joe held the towel as if he were a bullfighter and Wishbone were a charging bull. "All right, all right, enough is enough!" Joe said. Laughing, Joe tossed the towel over Wishbone. Everything went dark for Wishbone, and everything smelled like terry cloth. Wishbone spun in a circle. Joe got his hands on the towel-covered dog at last. "Would you please hold still? Just let me give you a good rub."

Wishbone settled down, enjoying the attention and the massage. "Sorry, Joe." Wishbone arched his back under the thick towel as Joe bore down on him, rubbing vigorously and laughing.

"That's much better!" Ellen said from behind Joe, her hands on her hips. "Honestly, Joe, how did you two get so wet?" The storm had died down, but gusts of wind still dashed rain against the windows. Ellen ran her hand through her son's hair. "Wishbone looks better. Now, you march right upstairs and take a nice hot shower!"

"Oh, Mom!"

"Don't 'Oh, Mom' me, young man! You just got over the flu, and I don't want you getting sick again. Now, march! I'll finish here."

Joe rose reluctantly to his feet, paused, then shook his head, sending rainwater all over his mother.

She raised her hands, laughing. "Joe!"

With a grin, Joe replied, "Well, it worked for Wishbone."

Wishbone, feeling drier, grinned, too. "It's like I always say—humans *can* be taught."

Ellen pointed toward the stairs. "Go!"

"Okay, Mom."

Joe headed out of the room toward the stairs, wet pant legs squishing together as he walked. Wherever he went, water puddled up in drippy footsteps.

Ellen reached down for the towel, and Wishbone pawed her leg. "The dog is still damp, Ellen. A little more towel action, if you please." As Ellen began, Wishbone sighed happily. "Oh, that's good!"

Ellen rubbed away, still shaking her head. Finally, she wrapped Wishbone in another dry towel and left him curled up by the fireplace, his black nose poking out.

Okay, this is better, Wishbone thought, as he snuggled deeper into his towel. Somehow, he found it really restful to stretch out in front of the fireplace, even if it was the middle of the summer and there was no fire. From upstairs he could hear the water gush as Joe took his shower.

Around the corner in the kitchen, Ellen bustled with pots and pans, getting dinner under way. Wishbone relaxed and sighed.

This is the life, he thought happily. *This is just what a dog needs to do some heavy mental digging. Dig, dig, dig. Think think, think!* The image of Mr. Faulkner floated to the surface of his mind, the bird's red eyes staring at something beyond Wishbone's vision. Wishbone couldn't understand why Joe was attracted to that bird. Yet, day after day, Joe fed Mr. Faulkner, gave him water, and changed his paper, and—most digusting of all—scratched his head and talked to him.

A dog would never stoop so low as to reach up and pet a bird. Hmm . . . that didn't sound right, somehow. Anyway, that crazy old parrot knew something, Wishbone was sure of that. The Jack Russell terrier stared thoughtfully at the empty fireplace. *And I'd know it, too, if I could just figure out what that irritating bird was squawking about!*

Joe felt better after his hot shower. He changed into dry clothes and came downstairs to dinner. He helped himself to stuffing, gravy, and a drumstick from the roast chicken Ellen had prepared. He reached for a tempting ear of corn on the cob.

Watching him, Ellen said, "Take some Brussels sprouts, too, Joe."

"Yes, Mom." Joe sighed, reluctantly spooning a very small serving of the green vegetable onto his plate.

Ellen added a few more Brussels sprouts to Joe's portion. "And don't try slipping them to Wishbone. He never eats them. He just hides them in the furniture, and then I have to find them and throw them away."

Joe glanced down at Wishbone, who was staring at the Brussels sprout on his fork with a mild look of doggie disgust. "You've been hiding them in the furniture?" he asked. "I thought you were at least burying them in Ms. Gilmore's flowerbeds."

Wishbone shook himself in an action that looked like a shrug.

Resigned, Joe bit into a Brussels sprout. It didn't taste *that* bad.

"There," Ellen said with a smile. "You've eaten a green vegetable and you didn't die."

"Not yet, anyway." Joe looked over at his mother. "But maybe it's a delayed poison, like in those mysteries where you eat something one day, and a week later everyone's trying to figure out why you aren't moving!"

Ellen poured herself a glass of milk. "Very funny. I assure you that if children were dropping dead from Brussels sprout poisoning, I'd have heard about it—and we'd be having spinach, instead."

Joe shuddered with mock horror and speared another Brussels sprout with his fork. "These are just fine, Mom. Mmm."

As they ate, Ellen asked about the break-in. Joe explained that Mr. Gurney still hadn't found anything missing, and that Officer Krulla didn't seem to think there was much chance of catching the burglar.

Ellen nodded. "And you're still finding mysterious books while you're reshelving?"

Joe nodded. "Five so far. Three of them were autographed, and all of them were first editions. Mr. Gurney says they're all in good condition or better. That means they're not stained, they have all their pages, and the bindings aren't split or frayed. Two of them have dust jackets in almost mint condition. They're a little worn at the edges, but otherwise, they're just like new—" Joe broke off. Something was nagging at him.

"What is it, Joe?" Ellen asked.

He shook his head. He had almost thought of something, but it had escaped him. "I don't know. I'm reading that book of Dad's. It reminds me of all this, somehow."

"The Haunted Bookshop?" Ellen asked. "In that one, the book turns out to be—"

"Please, Mom!" Joe blurted out in alarm. "I haven't finished it! I want to find out how it turns out myself!"

Ellen smiled. "Sorry. I've been a librarian long enough to recognize that look. I won't give away the ending, I promise."

Chapter Eight

By bedtime the storm had passed. The Talbot house was quiet and dark, except for where the full moon poured its beams in the windows, leaving pale phantom spots across the floor and furniture . . .

And except for the light that leaked from under Joe Talbot's bedroom door.

A sleepless Joe sat up in bed, pillows stuffed behind his back, and his sheets and bed covers all over the floor. His reading lamp shone over his shoulder and onto the book propped up against his knees. At the foot of his bed, Wishbone lay curled in a tight little circle. Occasionally, as the pages turned, his ears twitched as if to say "Bedtime *is* bedtime," and a soft doggie sigh escaped him.

Joe's eyes strayed to his clock. *Twelve-ten in the morning! I should be asleep,* he thought. Then his fingers turned another page.

The Haunted Bookshop was an old book, just like the ones he'd been shelving for Mr. Gurney. No one would mistake it for a rare volume, though. Its pages were dog-eared and worn. It had probably been old even when Joe's dad first bought it, and it had seen much hard use. Using his thumb as a bookmark, Joe closed the book and ran his finger over the embossed title.

The Haunted Bookshop.

He'd started reading the book as soon as he'd brought it home. Now he was getting into the exciting parts, where someone kept breaking into the store. Whoever it was played strange tricks with one book—sometimes it was missing, and sometimes it showed up in the store again.

It's really strange, Joe thought as he carefully turned another page. *This book is just like what's happening at Rendezvous Books.* Christopher Morley's tale was set in the New York City of 1919. The kindly, elderly owner of a bookshop called Parnassus (but more familiarly known as the Haunted Bookshop) was baffled when one of his books vanished. There was even a bookstore dog, a faithful old animal who slept right in the store.

As Joe read, he frowned. He was certain the book was telling him *what* was happening—the problem was still *why.* Joe had the annoying feeling that he almost understood—almost, but not quite. If he could just get it all into focus, it would be clear. . . .

At the foot of the bed, Wishbone opened his mouth in a jaw-cracking yawn, stretched, and wandered up to Joe's side. He found an empty spot, turned around a few times to make it perfect, and settled into another circle. This time, however, his eyes stayed open, moving sadly from Joe to the light and back again.

"Okay, okay, Wishbone." Joe laughed, looking at him. "I can take a hint. It's time to go to sleep!" He started to reach for the light, then hesitated. He looked again at the inscription on the flyleaf:

This book belongs to
Stevie Talbot—
Grade 6.

Softly, Joe said, "This was my dad's book when he was a kid, Wishbone—when he was a kid just like me, just like all the kids who used to own Mr. Gurney's books."

Wishbone pressed his cold nose against Joe's hand.

Joe smiled, tucked a bookmark into *The Haunted Bookshop,* and turned out the light. In a sleepy voice, he said, "I'll bet he was a great kid, Wishbone. He sure was a great dad."

Then Joe closed his eyes, one arm around a small snuggling dog, the other around an old worn book. *I'm going to solve this book mystery . . .* he thought, just before he drifted off to sleep. *I'll solve this with Wishbone and David and Sam . . . and Dad.*

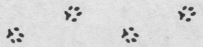

Wishbone loved to run. He especially loved to race Joe. "Come on, Joe! Betcha I get there first! Wish I knew where we were going!" It was early in the afternoon on

Sunday, and Wishbone ran alongside Joe's bike as they both raced toward downtown Oakdale. Joe had risen later than usual—"That's what happens when you stay up all night!"—dragged himself into the shower, and finally made it down to breakfast. Ellen had smiled knowingly at him as he laid the old book down beside his cereal bowl and started to eat.

Wishbone ran ahead of the bike, remembering how long he'd had to sit beside his empty food dish. "You were so tired you almost forgot to feed the dog, Joe! Clues are clues, but let's not forget the important things in life!"

After breakfast, Joe had called Sam and David and asked them to meet him later at the ballpark. In the early afternoon, Joe and Wishbone set off—not for the ballpark right away, but in the direction of Elm Street instead.

The storm of the night before was gone, but its effects still remained. The streets were spangled with fallen leaves, and even a few small branches had been stripped from the trees. Joe rode through puddle after puddle, while Wishbone leaped over them or ran around. "It's a good day for a run, Joe, but I hope there's some kind of reason for all this!"

Finally, they pulled up in front of a cozy-looking cottage on Elm Street. Joe parked his bike and hurried across the porch to knock on the door, with Wishbone sniffing away beside him.

"Yum! Joe, someone's having snacks in there— maybe he'll share with the dog. You think so?"

"Mr. Gurney!" Joe called, knocking loudly on the door again.

The door opened, and a blinking Kilgore Gurney peered at him. "Joe! What are you doing here? Not that I'm not glad to see you, but it *is* Sunday, and the store's closed. Come in, come in. Quentin and I are just having a light lunch and working on our game. . . ."

Wishbone tried to look hungry. "Did someone say . . . *lunch?*"

Joe gasped, trying to catch his breath. He and Wishbone stepped inside, where Dr. Quarrel sat in an armchair, hovering over a chessboard and holding a sandwich in his hand. He raised his eyebrows and said, "Well, hello."

Joe returned his greeting. Then he said, "I hate to bother you on your day off, Mr. Gurney, but I have an important question to ask you!"

Mr. Gurney exchanged a glance with Dr. Quarrel, who quickly pulled back his hand from the chessboard. "I saw you rearrange the men, Quentin," Mr. Gurney remarked. To Joe, he said, "Certainly, my boy, certainly. What can I tell you?"

Joe was still panting. From the floor, Wishbone looked up critically. "You've almost got it right, Joe. Stick your tongue out about three more inches and get more lung action into it." He looked around, sniffing. Mr. Gurney's house had bookcases everywhere, all stuffed with volumes from paperbacks to big hardcovers. That figured. A deeper sniff told Wishbone that lunch consisted of ham sandwiches—an interesting prospect!

Joe gasped and said, "You were going to check all the old records. Have any of the books we found showed up in them?"

Mr. Gurney looked thoughtful. "No. I've checked all my records as far back as ten years, and so far, the books haven't been listed."

"Not surprising," added Dr. Quarrel. "Those books probably have been kicking around the store since the days when your mother owned it."

Mr. Gurney made a shushing gesture. "I haven't found any of them listed," he said firmly. "It's quite a mystery."

Joe sounded excited when he replied, "It sure *is* a mystery, sir! That's the whole idea! Thanks, Mr. Gurney. 'Bye, Dr. Quarrel!"

And Joe was gone, hurrying through the doorway.

"Hey, Joe, they might offer us a sandwich!" Wishbone sighed and stood up to follow his friend out of the cottage, though he heard the next few words spoken by Mr. Gurney and Dr. Quarrel.

"What was that all about, Kilgore?" Dr. Quarrel asked in his grumbling voice.

"I haven't the slightest idea, Quentin, I haven't the slightest— Excuse me, since when does this game have three black rooks?"

By that time, Wishbone was outside and accelerating after Joe's bike.

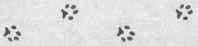

Joe was sweating and breathing hard. He felt as if he had just come off the basketball court after a vigorous practice. He cycled into Jackson Park, past the ball field, where two softball teams were warming up. Nearby was a family area with picnic tables, sandboxes, and playgrounds. Joe coasted toward a clump of oaks at the far end. There, under the towering shade trees, Samantha and David sat sprawled at a picnic table, waving at him.

Joe pulled up and parked his bike next to theirs. "Hi, guys!"

"Hi, yourself," Sam called back, tossing him a soda from the small cooler next to her. David had designed a special rack for the cooler on the back on her bike. Joe

noticed that even though Sam was off-duty, she was still wearing her Pepper Pete's hat.

Joe popped the pull tab on the can and took a big drink. The soda was cold and delicious. "Boy, that really hits the spot! Sure is a hot day."

"Just wait," said David, from where he lay across the top of the table. "Radio says it's going to be up in the nineties today. So what's the big news?"

Wishbone came trotting up, found a spot of shade, and collapsed, his tongue hanging out. Sam reached way down to scratch his ears. She looked up and asked, "Yeah, Joe, why'd you want us to meet?"

Excited, Joe sat on the picnic table bench and said, "I've found a new clue in the break-in! It's in that book I'm reading."

"Cool!" Sam said, sitting up straight. Then she grinned. "Well, actually it's hot, but a *clue* would be very cool."

David leaned back against the table. "I thought the clues would have been washed out of the alley by the rain. What kind of clue did you find in the book?"

"This kind." Joe proudly presented the old book. The two other kids gathered around him, the heat momentarily forgotten as they stared at the battered black cover.

"Is it from the bookstore?" David asked, taking it into his hands. "It looks old."

Joe shook his head. "No, it's mine. Mr. Gurney gave it to me. It's one of my dad's old books from when he was in the sixth grade."

"Is there something secret written in it?" David was carefully turning the brittle, yellowing pages, as if he were looking for hidden messages or secret codes.

Laughing, Joe said, "I don't think so. Anyway, the clue is in the story, not what anyone's added to it. Look at the title. It's *The Haunted Bookshop!*"

"You think the books were all messed up by a ghost?" Sam asked skeptically, frowning under her baseball cap. "Isn't that a little farfetched?"

With an exaggerated sigh, Joe said, "Maybe it would be if that was what I thought, but it isn't. And the haunted bookshop in the book isn't *really* haunted. That's the whole point!"

"I'm sorry, but you lost me on that last one," David said, frowning.

Joe took the book back and opened it to a chapter near the end. "Look, guys, remember how we talked about how weird this whole thing was? How whoever broke into Rendezvous Books didn't seem to actually *take* anything, just mess everything up? Remember how we laughed about how instead of finding anything missing, we just kept finding stuff, period?"

Sam nodded patiently. "We know all that, Joe. What we don't know is what this old book has to do with it."

David looked as if he agreed. "I'm with Sam. What's the point?"

"*The Haunted Bookshop* is all about a bookstore where the same book is stolen and secretly returned over and over again. Sometimes someone sneaks the book out, but at other times someone sneaks the book back *in!*"

Sam frowned again. "You mean, you think someone stole the books—"

"—and then broke in to bring them back?" David finished, his mouth hanging open in amazement.

"No!" Joe said. "But what if someone is breaking in not to *take* books, but just to *leave* them?"

"Joe, what are you talking about?" asked Sam. "That's not how burglary works."

"Exactly," Joe crowed triumphantly. "It's not burglary at all. It's—it's *unburglary!* It explains where those five books we found really came from!"

"Oh, come on, Joe," Sam grumped. "That doesn't make any sense! The ones you found weren't just ordinary books. They were autographed, or first editions, or something. They were all valuable. Why would someone do something like that?"

Joe tried to keep his voice calm as he said, "I don't know, Sam. That's what we have to figure out! Look, the big deal is that now we know something others don't. They're investigating the wrong crime. They think it's a burglary."

"And we think it *isn't* a burglary?" David remarked, looking uncertain.

Joe grinned. "Sure! Burglary is when someone breaks in and *takes* things. If I'm right, someone is breaking into Mr. Gurney's and *leaving* things!"

With a skeptical expression, Sam said, "So instead of breaking and *entering,* it's really breaking and *leaving?"*

Joe closed the book. "Right!" His spirits fell as the other two continued to stare at him. "I might be wrong," he admitted reluctantly. "Still, what if I'm not? That would explain a lot!"

Sam propped her face in her hands. "Well, I'd say it makes it all clear as mud."

"Okay," said David. "Let's start at the beginning. What's the reason for the book being returned in *The Haunted Bookshop?"*

"It's really neat. The book takes place after World War One. In the end, it turns out that enemy spies have been leaving coded messages in one particular book in the store. One spy would leave a message, and then another would take the book, decode the message, write a reply, and return the book to the store. That way the spies never had to contact each other in person, so it would be harder to catch them. The bad guys had a plan to set off a bomb at a peace conference."

Sam shook her head. "I don't think there's any peace conference going on in Oakdale."

Joe had to admit that Sam had a point. "Well, it's not spies in this case, but I do think someone's been leaving books in Mr. Gurney's store."

The kids and Wishbone sat in silence for a minute. Joe felt a touch of disappointment. International spies in Oakdale—that would have been a *real* mystery!

After a second, David said hopefully, "I don't suppose any of the new books have disappeared?"

Joe shook his head. "Nope—at least not in the way you mean. Yesterday, Mr. Gurney sold them all to a book dealer named Jack Brisco."

"Okay," David said. "Maybe you're right."

Joe shrugged. "I think so. Where else could the books have come from?"

Sam said, "Well, you keep telling us how Mr. Gurney's records aren't very complete. Maybe they were there all along."

"Maybe I'm wrong," Joe said. "We do need to investigate, though. That's how we'll find out for sure. We'll go back to the bookstore and look for those clues—unless you have something better to suggest."

Sam looked at David. David looked at Sam. Then they both looked at Joe, and Sam said, "Nope. Let's go take a look."

"Great!" Joe went to his bike. "We'll all ride over to the bookstore and take a good look around in the daylight and see what we can find!"

Chapter Nine

Joe enjoyed the ride over to Rosie's Rendezvous. The Sunday traffic was very light as they sped along. Wishbone ran after them, eyes intent and tongue dangling out. The heat was increasing with the day, and the puddles left over from the storm were beginning to evaporate. The air was moist and heavy when they finally stopped in the shade of the tree that stood in front of Rosie's Rendezvous.

"Wow! They weren't kidding about it being hot today, were they?" Joe panted, wiping the sweat from his face with his sleeve.

"Maybe it'll be cooler in the alley," Sam said, getting off her bike. "At least it's shadier there."

"Right," Joe said. "Let's go."

With Wishbone in the lead, the three slowly walked their bikes to the entrance of the alley. Even under the noon sun, the narrow alley was shadowy. The distant garbage cans hunched up against the building walls like hibernating bears. The kids stood there for a moment.

"You know," Sam said thoughtfully, "I think this place is even creepier in the daylight."

"We're going to have to go into the alley to look—

we can't just do it from out here." David peered into the shadows.

Even Joe felt doubtful. "Well, maybe we could *start* out here. . . . Wishbone! Come back here! Wishbone!" Joe called loudly. But he was too late. Wishbone had already charged into the alley.

Wishbone was excited to be back in the alley. "All right! Let's get going here! There are clues to find! Scents to smell! Snap to it, gang!" Trotting briskly across the rough pavement, Wishbone avoided the puddles that still lurked in the shadows. The kids leaned their bikes up against one of the walls and followed Wishbone.

"So, Sam, you see any clues?" Joe whispered.

"I can't see anything yet," she whispered back.

"Could I ask a question?" David said. "Why are we whispering? Is that really the rule for alleys?"

Joe and Sam both laughed.

Wishbone was sniffing around the back door of Rosie's. He looked over his shoulder at his friends. "It's a good thing you guys have a great bookstore dog like me to get things under way, or we'd be here all day!" He lowered his nose to investigate a pile of wet debris splashed up against one of the old brick walls. "Whoa! Lots of neat smells here. That's a good one . . . and that one . . . and that one. . . . I'll have to come back to that last one. Check out the trash, guys—that's where the best clues will be!"

Sam squatted down in the middle of the dark asphalt and stared at the glistening surface. "The rain must have poured down through here. This place is almost washed clean."

Wishbone yelped. "Wrong spot, Sam! Over here! Over here!"

"The middle may be clean, but the edges sure aren't," David said, pointing to the right. "There's a slight slant here, so all the rainwater ran downhill. All the loose trash got washed up against the walls. Oh, gross—what is this stuff? Yuck!"

Wishbone was turning it over with his nose. "Exactly right, David! This is prime yuck!"

"Okay," said Joe. "Okay, let's think now. We're on the downhill slant, so even if the burglar came from up the alley, any clues would have still ended up down here."

David nodded. "So maybe we should start over by the door and work our way out and see what's out of the ordinary."

Wishbone finally decided that the trash he was investigating held no clues—just unusually fragrant bits and pieces of this and that. "Good idea, guys! You check out the yuck, and I'll check out the building. Teamwork—that's the ticket. Stick with me and we'll have this solved by afternoon snack time! . . . Okay, well . . . by dinner, tops!" Abandoning the small pile of trash, Wishbone trotted over to the back door and began to sniff around.

The kids started to pick through the matted newspapers and old bottles and cans that lay up against the walls.

Carefully, Wishbone checked the heavy, old service door that led into Rosie's Rendezvous. There was something about it, something that tickled his nose like the beginning of a sneeze. Close—he was close, but no dog biscuit. Reluctantly, he moved away from the old door. He went on down the side of the building, pausing beside the low basement window. Its broken glass had been replaced, and through the new pane, Wishbone could dimly glimpse inside.

The Jack Russell terrier began to sniff and nose about. "All right, let me get my sharp canine mind to work here. Team it up with my sharp canine nose."

Finally, he came to the base of the window, and the scent of fresh putty slapped him right across the nose.

"Whoa! Jackpot!" Wishbone began to jump up and down and bark. His loud yelps bounced back and forth between the looming brick walls.

"Hey, Wishbone!" Joe said, running over to the excited dog. "You find something, boy? Is it a clue?"

Wishbone thumped his tail. "Good going, Joe! Think like a dog!"

Sam and David joined Joe and Wishbone. They all looked at the window the dog was barking at. It was about three feet long by two feet tall, below eye level, and they all crouched to peer at it.

"Is this the window he broke to get in?" Sam asked.

"It must be," Joe said. He poked his finger into the

spot where the windowpane joined the frame. "See, the putty is still soft."

Wishbone barked again. "Look on the ground!"

Joe leaned back. "This window is also clean. All the others are grimy and sealed with old paint. Yeah, the burglar came in here, all right. I guess someone had the glass replaced."

Wishbone barked again. Then he ducked his head to nose at scraps of soggy cardboard. "Look here, Joe! You're on a roll! Don't overlook this!"

Joe bent down to pull Wishbone back. "Better be careful, boy. That looks like glass there. . . . Hold on a minute!"

Sam leaned over to see. "What is it, Joe? Is it a clue?"

"I don't know if it's a clue, Sam, but it sure is a lot of glass—a lot of *broken* glass. Careful, guys."

"There's more of it down here," David called from farther down the wall. "The rain must have washed it up against Rosie's with the rest of the garbage."

Joe looked at the heap. "Hold on, hold on—stop barking, please, Wishbone!—there's something very strange here. . . ."

Wishbone pawed at his friend's pants leg. "That's right! Go for it, Joe!"

"Wishbone!" Joe stood up. "You know, there's enough broken glass here to make a whole pane of the window."

Sam and David nodded mutely.

Sounding thoughtful, Joe said, "When something hits a window, some of the glass falls on the side where it's hit, but not all of it. If Rosie's was broken *into,* then shouldn't the broken glass be on the *inside?* You guys see what this means?"

"I get it," Sam said slowly. "That means the burglar didn't break the window from the outside."

"It means he broke it from the *inside*," David continued. "Maybe he just pushed hard against a pane until it fell out and shattered."

Wishbone turned a backflip. "Eureka!"

The kids stood and stared at the new window, clean above the dull, streaked shards of broken glass that glinted in the wet rubbish below it.

"All right," Joe said slowly. "The window was broken by someone on the inside. Okay. But who would have been in there, and how did he get in if he didn't come in through the window?"

"Gee," Sam muttered. "I thought clues were supposed to *help* you solve mysteries, not make them more mysterious."

Wishbone had moved back to the door and was sniffing away again. He paused to glance at Sam. "We just don't have *enough* clues yet—that's our problem." Wishbone stared up at the painted-over door window, his ears perked up and his eyes bright. "Hey, there's something else! Look out, guys!" A low growl escaped his throat, and the kids turned to him.

Joe followed Wishbone's gaze. "Have you found another clue, boy?"

Wishbone didn't look around. "Just listen, Joe. That's why I'm not barking! Just listen!"

The kids stood in the cool shade and listened. Even muffled by the door, there was no mistaking the harsh voice that screamed on the other side.

"Awk! Write what you know! Awk! Write what you know! Awk!"

"That's Mr. Faulkner!" Joe cried.

"*William* Faulkner?" David questioned, sounding thoroughly confused.

Joe shook his head. "No! Mr. Gurney's parrot! I told

you about him! Something's got him really upset!" Joe leaned forward to put his ear against the metal door, and it moved. "Hey!" Joe said, surprised. "This door's supposed to be locked, but—" He tugged the handle. Silently, on well-oiled hinges, it swung open, revealing the dark interior of the closed gift shop. A breath of air conditioning wafted out into the alley, chilling them all.

"But it *isn't* locked," Sam muttered, her voice sounding uneasy.

"What are you kids doing back here?" The voice snapped out of the alley like a pistol shot. Feeling as if he'd received a sudden electrical shock, Joe twirled around. Someone loomed up tall and lean, backlit by the sunlight at the very end of the alley.

"Who's that?" Joe called, only a slight quiver in his voice. Sam and David pressed in on either side behind him, and Wishbone growled at his feet. Whatever they were going to face, they were going to face it together.

"I asked first." Jack Brisco stepped into view. Dark sunglasses covered his eyes, and his brilliant white teeth gleamed as he smiled. "Mr. Gurney's helper, isn't it?"

Breathing a sigh of relief, Joe said, "That's right, sir. I work for Mr. Gurney. I'm Joe Talbot. These are my friends David and Samantha."

Mr. Brisco nodded to the others. "I'm pleased to meet you. Isn't the store closed on Sundays?"

Joe pointed. "It is, Mr. Brisco, but there's something wrong. The back door's open—"

"Jack? What's going on back there?" A young woman's voice came drifting down the alley. Mary Benson, the clerk who worked at Rosie's, suddenly appeared behind

Jack Brisco. She was wearing a light flower-patterned summer dress, and her hair was all done up. "Oh, hi, Joe. What are you doing here?"

Joe thought he could ask her and Jack the same question. "We were just looking around," he said.

Mary smiled. "We were driving past the store and saw your bikes out front, so we stopped to see who was here."

A thought flashed through Joe's mind: *Mary has a key to Rosie's.* Joe, Sam, and David had been wondering how the burglar had gotten inside to break the window out—but Joe would never have suspected Mary. He liked her, and he felt his heart sink a little at the thought that she might be involved in the break-in.

"Joe's doing a good deed, it seems," Jack Brisco said. "It appears that he and his friends have made a sinister discovery. The back door to your shop is unlocked."

Mary stepped forward, frowning. "Unlocked? It can't be. I checked it myself—" Mary's hand flew to her mouth. "Oh, dear, you don't think there's been another break-in, do you?"

"I'd say it's a distinct possibility." Jack Brisco paused thoughtfully. "I suggest that you go and call Mr. Gurney. If his shop's been burglarized again, he needs to know immediately."

"And we need to call the police," Joe said. For the merest second it seemed to him that Jack Brisco's smile slipped the slightest bit.

Mr. Brisco nodded. "You're right. We do need to call the police. There seems to be a lot of crime here for such a quiet neighborhood. Let me make sure no one is inside. I can call the police from the store. Wait here for me." His lips gently brushed Mary's cheek, and she blushed a bright pink.

Mr. Brisco went carefully into the store, switching on a light. He stood just inside, between the employee break room on his right and the rest rooms on his left.

"It looks empty," he called back. "Maybe I'd better not go upstairs until the police come over to check. Mary, where's the phone?"

"The front counter," Mary said.

Brisco vanished into the store.

A few minutes later he came back. "The police are on the way," he announced. "Mary, we'd better wait around in front. There might be questions. Joe, you and your friends will stay, won't you?"

"Yes, sir," Joe assured him.

"Good. And while I'm thinking about it " He reached into his jacket and produced a cream-colored envelope. He held it out. "When you see Mr. Gurney, please thank him for the books he's found for me. This is a list of some others I'd like him to keep his eyes open for—some mysteries, and a children's book. Same terms as before—cash on delivery."

Joe took the offered envelope. Just then Wishbone growled at Mr. Brisco's feet.

Brisco glanced down, his smile wide. Then he looked back at Joe. "Nice dog, Joe. Come on, Mary." With that, he and Mary walked back up the alley and turned toward the street. As soon as the two were gone, all three kids breathed a sigh of relief.

"Wow!" David said. "So that's Jack Brisco."

"I don't trust him," Joe replied, thinking furiously. "He's *got* to be mixed up with this somehow. All the extra books we found just *happened* to be on his first list. I think there's something really suspicious about Mr. Jack Brisco."

"I don't see how he could be involved," Sam said. "He's the one who *bought* those valuable books from Mr. Gurney, remember?"

"Joe," David said, "what about Mary?"

Joe felt funny again—as if he were finding out things he didn't want to know. "I see what you mean," he said slowly. "I thought of it, too. Mary works in Rosie's, and someone broke the window out from the inside. But she *likes* Mr. Gurney. Anyway, she'd lose her job if anyone thought she was breaking windows and messing up the bookstore."

From the open door, the cold air from the dark interior of the store brushed their necks, and the harsh voice of Mr. Faulkner now rang out clear as a cracked bell.

"Awk! Write what you know! Awk! Write what you know!"

Chapter Ten

Joe turned and peered into the shop. Wishbone was sniffing away near Joe's feet. Joe bit his lip, wondering if the burglar might be upstairs at that very moment. He didn't notice Wishbone slipping inside until he heard the sound of toenails on the staircase.

"Wishbone!" Joe said urgently. "Come back!"

"Oh, man," David said. "He's going to get in trouble."

"Come on," Joe muttered. "We'd better go in and get him."

"Inside?" Sam asked, eyeing the dark store suspiciously.

"I don't know," David said. "Mr. Brisco told us to stay out here until the police came."

"I've got to get Wishbone," Joe said firmly. He started to go into the dark store. "Where are you, boy?" he called softly. At the top of the stairs, the bookstore door was open. Joe started to go up, hoping he wasn't about to run into more trouble than he could handle.

Halfway up the steps, Joe heard Sam and David coming inside, and he breathed a sigh of relief.

"Glad you decided to join me," he said.

From the foot of the stairs, Sam said, "We decided it was spookier outside than inside."

Still, Joe felt relieved. Brisco had turned off the light when he left the store, and Rosie's Rendezvous Books & Gifts boutique was pretty eerie without any lights on. The display cases and shelves seemed to lurk in the gloom, vague and indistinct. Joe must have been in the gift shop a dozen times, but in the dark, nothing looked the way it should. The breeze from the air conditioner should have cooled him off. Instead, it just sent a nervous chill over his whole body.

Silently, the kids slipped up the staircase into the darkness. Joe swallowed hard. Could the burglar still be there, waiting for them in the shadows at the top of the stairs? There was only one way to find out. Pausing for a moment on the landing to work up his courage, Joe gently swung the heavy, old oak door wide open and stepped inside the bookstore.

"Boy, it sure is dark up here," David whispered. The windows, down past shelves of books, didn't allow much light to reach the sales counter. The tall shelves could be hiding anything in the shadows between them.

From beyond the shelves, Mr. Faulkner screeched loudly, "Awk! Write what you know! Awk! Write what you know! Awk!"

Joe fumbled on the wall beside the door. "The light switch is over here . . . someplace." He finally found the switch, and he paused again. Would turning on the light reveal something horrible? Was it better to keep whatever it was in the dark? Taking a deep breath, Joe finally worked up enough courage to flick the switch.

The overhead lights blazed, flooding Rendezvous Books with illumination.

Joe heard Sam gasp, and David groaned, "Oh, man!"

Joe stared in shocked dismay, while his friends stood with their mouths wide open. To their right, in the Non-fiction sections, everything was just the way he had left it at noon on Saturday, the books filling their shelves in neat rows. But straight ahead, in the Fiction sections, the tall bookcases gaped blank and empty. On the floor stood stack after stack of books, the piles littering the aisles. The mysterious intruder had struck again! Wishbone suddenly peered around from behind one stack. He didn't look as if he were chasing a burglar.

"Look at this mess!" Sam exclaimed, sounding shocked.

Joe walked over to Wishbone, patted him, and looked at one of the stacks. "It isn't a mess, Sam."

David snorted. "Sure looks like a mess to me."

"Awk! Write what you know! Awk! Write what you know!" the parrot repeated.

Joe said, "I'd better see about Mr. Faulkner." He

103

walked over to the chess corner, where Mr. Faulkner teetered on his perch, glaring at him, his green wings outspread. He seemed to recognize Joe and folded his wings. Joe stroked the soft feathers on Mr. Faulkner's chest. In a soothing voice, he said, "It's okay, Mr. Faulkner, it's me." Joe felt something tug at his jeans leg. It was Wishbone, trying to pull him back down the aisle. "Just a minute, Wishbone. Let me calm down our friend."

From his perch, Mr. Faulkner spread his great dusty wings again. Sam and David had followed Joe. The parrot glared at the kids with his red eyes. He looked like some ancient griffin—an imaginary cross between an eagle and a lion—that had escaped from one of the books around him. His burning gaze swept over the group until his crimson eyes settled on Wishbone. Dog and bird stared at each other. Then, slowly, Mr. Faulkner settled back down on his perch. Like an old store awning lowering down, leathery lids slid over his baleful eyes and he grumbled back to sleep.

David said, "I think Wishbone just hypnotized him somehow."

Joe shook his head. "At least he's quiet. Quick, now, before anyone else comes upstairs. We have to get over to the Mystery shelves and see if we can spot the clues I think we'll find!"

Joe quickly led the others over to the Mystery section. He glanced at the haphazard stacks of books. He felt a surge of satisfaction when his suspicion proved true, and he turned, smiling, to his friends.

"Okay, guys, what does all this tell us?" Joe asked.

Sam gaped at him. "Huh?"

Joe gestured. "Just tell me what you see, all right?"

"Okay, okay," Sam said, looking around. "All the books in this section are off the shelves and on the floor."

With a laugh, Joe said, "Too obvious, Sam!"

Sam frowned. "What, then?"

"Oh, I get it!" David exclaimed, kneeling down to take a better look at the books. "Look, Sam, the burglar is taking care not to damage the books. All the books are closed and on their sides. None of them is opened. None of the pages is bent. An ordinary burglar wouldn't have been so careful."

Sam picked up a few books from one stack. "These are still in alphabetical order, too."

David ran his finger up the side of another stack. "These books are *all* stacked in alphabetical order!"

Joe nodded. "That's exactly right. And what does this fact tell us?"

"We're dealing with a really neat burglar!" Sam snapped.

Joe grinned at her. "Nope—just a really *careful* one. If the pages are torn or the spines damaged, the books would be worthless! Mr. Gurney taught me that. Whoever is doing this doesn't want Mr. Gurney to lose any money! Come on. The police will be up here in a minute, and before they come, I need you guys to help me take a quick look at these books."

David looked uncertain. "Why? What are we looking for?"

Feeling almost as if he were a real detective, Joe said, "Books."

Sam said, "Those should be easy to find! They're all over the place."

"But we're looking for books that *don't* belong here," Joe said, pulling out the list Jack Brisco had given him. "Mr. Brisco said he was looking for some mysteries and a children's book." Opening the unsealed envelope, Joe scanned the list. "Now, the first one is a first edition of a mystery, *The Murder of Roger Ackroyd,* by Agatha Christie, published in 1926. If I'm right, we should look here among the C's."

"So we're looking to make sure that the book is here," Sam said.

Joe shook his head. "No. If I'm right, we won't find it—not where it belongs, anyway."

David's expression was a look of confusion. "So we're looking for a book that isn't here. Okay, let's get started. This calls for some extra-hard looking!"

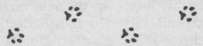

A keenly interested Wishbone watched as Sam, Joe, and David began to sort through books by Agatha Christie. Sam found two old paperback copies of *The Murder of Roger Ackroyd,* but the kids were searching for a very old hardcover. They had been searching for only a couple of minutes before they all froze at the sound of a siren coming from outside. They walked to the counter just as Mr. Gurney and Officer Krulla came in.

"What's going on here?" the policeman asked, as he stared at the kids.

"It's all right, Officer," Mr. Gurney said, puffing from his quick climb up the steps. "You remember Joe Talbot. He works here."

Wishbone pawed at Joe's leg. "Go ahead, Joe! Tell them your theory!"

Joe introduced his friends and said, "We came inside to get Wishbone. He just darted in. I think he was checking to make sure the burglar wasn't still up here."

Officer Krulla scratched his balding head. "Joe, you kids shouldn't be here—you're messing up a crime scene. Unless—"

Wishbone sensed what the policeman was about to say next.

"—unless you did it yourselves!"

Wishbone went to Joe's side and sat there, feeling protective. No one was going to accuse his best friend of such a criminal act!

Mr. Gurney was shaking his head sadly. "Why would anyone do this? Why would anyone do it even once, let alone twice?"

"We don't think anything was taken," David said.

Joe cleared his throat. "Uh . . . Mr. Gurney, I—that is, my friends and I have a theory about what's happening."

Sitting at Joe's feet, Wishbone beamed. "Nice to be included, Joe. Tell him, tell him, tell him!"

Mr. Gurney stroked his white beard and glanced at Officer Krulla. "Well, I for one would be delighted to hear it. This whole thing has me about as frantic as a cat at a dog show."

Wishbone blinked. "A feline at a dog convention—now, that *is* a reason to be frantic!"

Joe said, "We don't think those valuable books have been lost at all. Someone's been secretly bringing them into the store."

Officer Krulla shook his head. "I've been on the force for a long time, Joe. I can tell you from experience, that's not the way burglary works."

Absent-mindedly, Mr. Gurney waved his hand at Officer Krulla in a shushing gesture. "Explain yourself, Joe."

Pointing toward the stacks of books, Joe said, "Whoever has been breaking in never steals anything. He never even messes anything up—not really. It's easy to pick up after him, but the confusion covers up the fact that hidden in the stacks of books are some new books—well, not really new, but valuable, books."

107

Mr. Gurney looked confused. His expression didn't surprise Wishbone. The idea was a big bone to chew on. Mr. Gurney frowned, thought, shrugged, and waited patiently for the rest of Joe's theory.

Joe took another deep breath and plowed on. "Okay, if that's right, then the books have to be hidden where they'd stand out—but not stand out *too* much. Anything that's new is going to be in the wrong section, so when we see it, we'll know it."

"That seems a bit obtuse, my boy."

Officer Krulla stared at Mr. Gurney. "Obtuse?"

Mr. Gurney tried again. "Um . . . obscure, opaque . . . er . . . um . . . confusing."

Joe said, "I think that's the whole idea, sir. Now, according to our theory, the next batch of new books won't be in Mystery, because it's one of the sections that has actually really been messed up. But we've got a secret weapon."

"Where's this weapon?" Officer Krulla asked, still looking as if he hadn't quite worked out *obtuse* yet.

"Right here," Joe said, pointing down. They all looked at Wishbone.

Wishbone grinned up at them. "That's me! Wishbone! Secret Weapon Dog in the war on crime!"

Joe explained, "Wishbone has been your Official Bookstore Dog for over a week, so he's got a good nose for what's supposed to be where. When I first found Ray Bradbury's *Dark Carnival,* it was because Wishbone was sniffing it—he seemed to know it was out of place. Maybe he can find anything else out of place, too."

Officer Krulla snorted, and Mr. Gurney said kindly, "You know, Joe, I have a great admiration for Wishbone, but don't you think that's expecting an awful lot from one little dog?"

108

Wishbone gave him a long stare. "Oh, ye Gurneys of Little Faith! And don't call me 'little.' I'm precisely the right size!"

Sam said, "Give him a chance, Mr. Gurney! I mean, what have you got to lose?"

Mr. Gurney nodded in agreement. He knelt down and scratched Wishbone behind the ears. Wishbone looked up at him encouragingly. "Yeah, give the little— oops, precisely-the-right-size—dog a chance, Mr. G. You might be surprised. In fact, I can almost guarantee it!"

Finally, Mr. Gurney sighed and got back to his feet. "Well, Officer, I say let him try."

Officer Krulla spread his hands. "It's your store, Mr. Gurney. Let's see the dog do his stuff."

"All right!" Joe said. He led Wishbone to the stacks and let him start sniffing the books. "Do it, Wishbone! Find the books that weren't here yesterday!"

Wishbone dashed away. "Clear the way! Secret Weapon Dog on the move!"

With the others hot on his heels, Wishbone ran halfway through the store, nose down and sniffing like crazy. He trotted from one pile of books to the next, taking deep sniffs of dusty-smelling books.

"That's it! Get the old nose to working! Old Rendezvous books smell like old Rendezvous books. Old books, old books . . . Whoa! That book smells like Joe! He must have shelved this one!"

Mr. Gurney and the kids had almost caught up with Wishbone when the terrier's ever-sensitive nose went up in the air. He paused for a moment, then charged toward the right.

"He's heading for the sorting room!" Mr. Gurney said, then puffed as he ran.

"Wishbone! Wait up, boy! Wishbone!" said Joe.

No time for that, Wishbone thought, as he scratched at the closed door of the sorting and storage room. *Whatever is new has to be in here.*

Mr. Gurney opened the door for him, and Wishbone rushed inside. The faint light from the distant windows made everything dark and shadowy. The air was thick with the smell of old books and dust and people—Joe, Mr. Gurney, Dr. Quarrel, and regular customers. Wishbone's nose led him to the Juvenalia sorting shelves, where Joe had spent many days unpacking and arranging all the new acquisitions.

Wishbone passed a spot, froze, then turned back. "Whoa! Wait a doggie minute! Something over . . . let's see . . . there! The noble dog strikes again! The Western sorting shelf! Right across from the kids' books! Sneaky, but not sneaky enough to fool the Official Bookstore Dog!" He pushed his nose in among the stacks of Western books, pawing at one in particular.

Joe and the others came running in from behind Wishbone. Joe bent down. "What did you find, boy?"

Wishbone nosed the stack and it toppled, leaving one book exposed. "Wrong book with the wrong smell in the wrong place!" Wishbone looked up triumphantly.

Joe reached past Wishbone and hefted the large book. It was noticeably bigger than the copies of Zane Grey novels that made up the rest of the pile. Everyone crowded around him as he handed it over to Mr. Gurney.

Mr. Gurney patted around his coat pockets until he located two black pawns, a tin of cough drops, and a pair of wire-rimmed spectacles that he slipped over his nose. "Well, this is certainly misfiled. Very good, Wishbone. It should have been on the other side of the aisle."

"What is it, sir?" David asked, pushing in between Joe and Sam. Officer Krulla peered over their heads.

Turning the big book over in his hands, Mr. Gurney said, "Well, it seems to be a nice first edition of *The Wonderful Wizard of Oz*. No foxing, a little fading on the spine." He flipped the book open to the front and squinted. Then his eyes grew large behind his spectacles and slowly, like a hot-air balloon deflating, Mr. Kilgore J. Gurney settled softly to the floor. "Oh, my stars!"

"Hey! Are you okay?" Officer Krulla asked.

"What is it, Mr. Gurney?" Sam questioned.

His eyes gleaming, Mr. Gurney looked up. He swallowed hard and said, "It's a truly wonderful find, my dear. It's a first edition of one of the greatest children's books of all time. But it's even more than that."

His shaky finger pointed to the title page. There, in neatly inked letters, was an inscription:

> To all children everywhere,
> But especially to all the Dorothys,
> From your friend,
> L. Frank Baum.

His voice trembling, Mr. Gurney said, "This was my favorite story when I was ten years old. I read it to my little sister. Her name is Dorothy, and—" He got up. "I'm going to mail this to her! She's a grandmother now, and I know she'd love to read this to her grandsons and granddaughter!"

Wishbone looked up proudly. "I hope they all have dogs! That's a great story about Toto."

Clutching the book to his chest and sounding as if he were close to tears of joy, Mr. Gurney said, "I can't believe I could have a book like this in my store and not have a record of it."

"You can't believe it, Mr. Gurney, because you *didn't* have it," Joe told him. "I've been working in this section for days, and that book wasn't on any shelf. Someone broke in and left it where we would eventually find it. And I think you could sell it if you wanted to."

"I don't want to," Mr. Gurney said, holding the book even tighter. "I don't even want to *look* for a customer."

"You wouldn't have to look far." Slowly, Joe took the cream-colored envelope out of his back pocket and handed it to Mr. Gurney. "You're going to find it listed right here."

Wishbone yipped. "Smart thinking, Joe! And here's something else you need to think about—remember the first time you heard Mr. Faulkner screech his advice about writing what you know? I do. It's something he says whenever Jack Brisco is around!"

Chapter Eleven

Joe couldn't help but feel proud of his quick thinking. He was pleased, too, at how happy Mr. Gurney was about finding *The Wonderful Wizard of Oz*.

Still clutching the book, Mr. Gurney told Officer Krulla that he had no wish to press charges against anyone yet. The policeman shrugged and left the store. Mr. Gurney finally put the book down on the counter, where he stared at it as if afraid it might vanish. At last he tore his gaze away, opened the cream-colored envelope, and looked through the list. "Right here," he said softly. "Someone is offering a lot of money for an autographed first edition of *The Wonderful Wizard of Oz*. You're right, Joe. Mr. Jack Brisco is somehow involved in this."

Sam asked Joe, "Why didn't you tell that to Officer Krulla?"

Joe shook his head. It was hard to explain, but he didn't want to get anyone in trouble—certainly not Mary Benson from downstairs, and not even Mr. Brisco. "I don't think I should," he said. "Mr. Gurney's the one to do that."

The bookstore owner sighed and ran his fingers through his white hair. "I just couldn't. Don't you see? Whoever is doing all this isn't really hurting anything. In fact, the books I sold Mr. Brisco last week brought in more money than a month of regular sales. It's helping the store, not hurting it."

"But it's wrong," David objected.

Mr. Gurney nodded and smiled. "You young people have come up with a wonderful theory and some astonishing proof to back it up. But there's another possibility. What if the books really *were* in the store all along, and the person breaking in just moved them around? What if it's a prank?"

Joe thought that over. "Someone would have to be pretty foolish to pull off a prank that involves breaking and entering."

Mr. Gurney folded the list and replaced it in its envelope. "Oh, I agree, I agree. But what if it's some young people and they get caught? If I report this and the police catch them—and they will, eventually—then Officer Krulla would have to arrest them. A police record is a terrible thing for a young person to have."

Joe felt frustrated. "But what if it isn't a prank, Mr. Gurney?"

Mr. Gurney shook his head. "I don't know what to do. I wish Quentin were here! He's always quick to offer advice!"

"Where is Dr. Quarrel, anyway?" Joe asked. "I thought he'd be here as soon as he knew there had been another break-in."

Mr. Gurney went to a case, unlocked it, and carefully put the copy of *The Wonderful Wizard of Oz* inside. "I doubt if he knows. After we finished lunch, Quentin told me he was going to the bus station to meet his grandson, who's in town for a visit." He sighed. "There's going to be a lot of work tomorrow."

David looked at Joe and Sam. He said, "Not necessarily.

We can all pitch in and put the books back on the shelves. They're still in order, anyway, so it won't be hard, with all of us helping."

"Sure," Sam said. "We'll be happy to help."

Wishbone barked. Joe said, "Maybe Wishbone can find some more out-of-place books."

Mr. Gurney agreed, and soon Rendezvous Books was a swarm of activity that barely paused when Mr. Gurney ordered another Pepper Pete's pizza—one that Sam didn't have to deliver, because it was her day off.

Sure enough, just as Joe had thought, strange books started to turn up. Joe found an Agatha Christie book misplaced in War Fiction, and Wishbone nosed out an autographed *Life on the Mississippi,* an autobiographical book by Mark Twain. Sam and David found an autographed Ellery Queen mystery, and another one by John Dickson Carr.

As the day wore on toward evening and the books flew back up on the shelves, one thought kept running around and around in Joe's mind: *What kind of kids have a stash of old books worth thousands of dollars to throw away on a prank?*

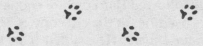

The next day, Wishbone was on the alert, prowling up and down the aisles of Rendezvous Books, looking for anything suspicious. Unfortunately, the way things had been going, everything looked suspicious! Together with Sam, Joe, and David, he had found six more strange books as the kids straightened up. All were first editions, and half of them were autographed. Even without *The Wonderful Wizard of Oz,* they were worth much more than a thousand dollars.

Wishbone wondered if maybe Mr. Gurney was right—what if the reverse burglars had been young people? Wishbone decided they'd have to be high school or college students. And they'd have to have a good knowledge of the store's physical layout. *Think, think, think! Dig, dig, dig! Whoa! Brainstorm, Wishbone, old dog! Suspicious older kids who haunt the bookstore? Come to think of it, I know at least two of them!*

For the remainder of the day, Wishbone would patrol the aisles, stopping at regular stations—the front desk, the chess game, Mr. Faulkner—and at regular people—the professor with the fig bars, the Romance lady, Joe. Finally, in the early afternoon, he was rewarded for his hard work. Harold Whittaker stood on the landing, peering nervously from side to side. Then he turned and walked in what he probably thought was a casual way in the direction of the History section.

Wishbone watched him as he turned down an aisle. The young man's eyes darted furtively all around, as if he were trying not to be noticed. Wishbone shook his head. *Boy, why doesn't Harold just wear a sign that says "Suspicious Person"?*

Wishbone followed Harold. Sure enough, the college student made a bee-line for the old copy of *The Decline and Fall of the Roman Empire*. He cradled it in his arms and then settled down to reading it. Wishbone settled down, too, resting his head on his paws. He was still settled there an hour later—and valiantly fighting the urge to take a quick nap—when he heard timid footsteps behind him. He looked up, and there was the young woman with the strawberry-blond hair.

Okay, the plot thickens! Now we'll see what we'll see! Oops. Or maybe not . . .

Because, unfortunately, she didn't do anything. She

just stood there staring at Harold and his book. When it became obvious that he wasn't going to put it down anytime soon, she sighed and turned away.

Silently, Wishbone followed her. She ended up in one of Mr. Gurney's large, old, overstuffed chairs. Quietly, she set down a paper bag—Wishbone's nose told him she had lunch inside it, a salad and a banana—and started leafing through a magazine and looking miserable.

After a minute, Wishbone yawned. *Well, this is about as interesting as watching a collie shed!*

Another hour dragged by, during which time the young woman looked at eight old magazines, checked on Harold and the book six times, and stared into space a lot. Finally, Wishbone decided it was time to take matters into his own paws. After all, as he had said before, faint heart never won fair squeak toy!

With a sudden leap, Wishbone burst out from behind

the bookcases and raced up to the overstuffed chair. The young woman heard his clattering claws and looked up, startled, just in time to see him snatch her lunch from the floor next to her. Then, with a bound, he was off and running through the stacks.

"Oh, no! My lunch!" a voice wailed behind him. Wishbone heard her jump up from her seat and come running after him.

Wishbone made a sharp right turn. This had to be timed just right. After all, lunch-snatching could ruin his reputation as Rendezvous Books's Official Bookstore Dog. Fortunately, the young woman didn't seem to want to disturb anyone by screaming—at least after that first outburst. "Good girl, good girl! Just follow the nice doggie, and everything's going to be fine!"

Then, just as she was about to catch up with him, they rounded a corner. There, on the floor, sat Harold, still engrossed in his book. He looked up just in time for Wishbone to run across his legs, and for the young woman to stumble over him. He dropped the book, jumped up, and caught her before she fell.

"Oh!" the girl said with a gasp. "I'm sorry!"

Harold's face was beet-red. "Excuse me," he muttered. "I didn't mean to trip you—"

"My lunch!"

They both looked down at Wishbone, who had dropped the paper bag and now sat staring sternly up at them. "Okay, kids, time to spill the literary beans! Are you, or are you not, the Mysterious Reverse Bookstore Burglars?"

Reaching down, Harold picked up the fallen bag. "Is this yours?"

The young woman, who was blushing as much as Harold, said, "Yes. That little dog—"

Wishbone was relishing his role as the Official Bookstore Dog. "Anything you say may be taken down and used against you in a court of law."

"—he stole my lunch!"

Wishbone blinked. "Uh . . . except that."

Harold said, "I think maybe he was just playing. Uh . . . excuse me, but, aren't you . . . uh . . . in, uh—"

The young woman adjusted her glasses. "What?"

Looking at her, Harold asked, "Uh . . . aren't you in Dr. Oettinger's Ancient History class?"

The young woman nodded. "Yes. I sit on the other side of the room from you."

Harold's face lit up with a big smile. Suddenly, he didn't seem nearly as awkward or angular. "I thought so! You're over by the window behind the girl with all the different headbands!"

"And you always sit in the back near the door." She smiled back at him.

Wishbone looked from one to the other and back again. "Whoa! Curiouser and curiouser!"

Harold held out his hand. "Harold Whittaker."

"Edith Wells," she said, taking it. "Harold, could I ask you a personal question?" He looked at her blankly and then nodded. She pointed at *The Decline and Fall*. "Are you through with that book? It's required reading, and by the time my paycheck comes in—"

"All the paperbacks and the used ones are gone, and the only texts left were new ones for sixty dollars, right?" He laughed at her startled look. "Same problem here. I work at the college computer center, and since the summer term has just started, we don't get paid until next Friday."

Edith laughed along with him. "I'm a server at the cafeteria, and I don't get paid until *Saturday!* I tried to get it from the library, but—"

"All the copies were checked out!" he said, finishing the sentence for her. "I've been coming here and trying to stay caught up with this copy of Mr. Gurney's— Oh, I bet that's what you were doing, too!"

Edith nodded shyly. "Uh-huh. Until I get paid, I can't afford to buy it."

Harold held the big book in his hands, looking down at it. "I've got an idea. How much money do you have right now?"

Edith opened her purse and dug around. At last she came up with a handful of crumpled bills. She carefully counted them out and held them up for him to see. It came to exactly nine dollars. "Lucky I can eat in the cafeteria for free," she said. "I'll be all right when my pay starts, but until then, this is it."

Harold grinned. "I've just got you beat. I have almost twelve. Let's go see what Mr. Gurney wants for the book—that is, if you think we could share it."

Wishbone followed them to the sales counter. There Mr. Gurney, his eyes bright, was reading through the treasured copy of *The Wonderful Wizard of Oz*. He looked up with a smile, taking off his reading glasses. "Yes?" he asked, in a dreamy voice that seemed as far away as Munchkinland or the Emerald City—or his own childhood.

"How much is this book, please?" Edith asked shyly.

Mr. Gurney looked at the book, then back at Harold and the young lady. He cleared his throat. "Well, hello, Harold. Nice to see you again. . . . Ordinarily, the book would sell for ten dollars, but this one's received a lot of use." Wishbone noticed how much Harold blushed at that, but Mr. Gurney didn't seem to pick up on the young man's expression. "Let's say, oh, five dollars."

Harold relaxed. "We can buy it together and still have a little money left until we get paid—that is, if you don't mind studying together . . . Edith?"

Softly, and with a smile, Edith said, "I think I'd like that . . . Harold."

Harold's face once again split into a transforming grin, and the two of them paid for the book. They walked very close together as they headed for the stairs.

Wishbone sighed. "Well, that didn't exactly solve the mystery, but, to coin a phrase, it looks like it might be the start of a beautiful friendship! Oh, well, I never really thought it was them, anyway—Harold was too single-minded, and Edith too nice. I guess the case is all back in Joe's hands again."

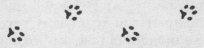

Just before noon on the following Saturday, brimming with impatience, Joe said, "Mr. Gurney? Can I talk to you for a minute?"

Mr. Gurney looked up from where he had been idly moving chess pieces around on the board. "Certainly, Joe. I seem to have a lot of time on my hands right now."

You really miss Dr. Quarrel, Joe thought, fighting back a smile. *It must be tough having to cheat at chess all by yourself.* Aloud, he said, "I've got an idea I think you might be interested in. Well, actually, we all had the idea—Sam and David and I."

With a chuckle, Mr. Gurney said, "Oh, a committee! I have to warn you, Joe, committees very rarely produce good ideas!"

"Well, sir, it's the only idea that we have. Look, Mr. Gurney, you don't want to call the police again, because whoever is doing this hasn't really hurt anyone—or anything—yet, right?"

Mr. Gurney folded his hands over his stomach. "Yes, that's basically correct. No harm done."

Joe took a deep breath. "Okay, but you want whoever it is to stop before getting into real trouble. So why don't we set a trap?"

Mr. Gurney took the black bishop out of the Discard slot and replaced it with a black rook. "Don't you think that sounds dangerous, Joe?"

Joe shook his head. "Not if you're right, Mr. Gurney. If it really is kids doing this mischief, we can keep them from getting in trouble with the police."

Mr. Gurney tilted back in his chair and thoughtfully stroked his white beard. "And what if it isn't kids?"

Seeing the interest in Mr. Gurney's eyes, Joe leaned forward. "We've thought of that, too. We'll hide out here with some snacks and drinks and see what happens. We'll put the phone where we're hiding, and we'll call the police if it's an adult. The break-ins have all been on weekend nights. What do you think, Mr. Gurney?"

Mr. Gurney looked thoughtful. "What makes you think the burglar is going to strike again?"

"Did Mr. Brisco give you another list this week?"

Mr. Gurney patted his pockets and produced a folded, cream-colored paper. "Yes. He bought the books we found—all except *The Wonderful Wizard of Oz*—and he left this list of seven more books. I don't have a single one of them in stock."

Joe took the list from Mr. Gurney and read through it. "Well, twice now someone has broken in over the weekend and left the very books Mr. Brisco needed. I think there's a good chance it will happen again."

Mr. Gurney ran his fingers through his beard again.

Then he slapped his fist down on the table, sending chess pieces spinning all over the place. "By Godfrey Daniels, I'll do it! I'll do it for two reasons. The first is so I can confront whoever is doing this and demand an explanation!"

Pleased at Mr. Gurney's agreement, Joe asked, "What's the second reason, sir?"

Mr. Gurney threw back his head and laughed long and loud. "Why, so I can tell Quentin Quarrel about all the fun he's missed when that old fossil finally gets back from traipsing around with his grandson!"

That afternoon, Joe felt exasperated when Ellen wouldn't hear of the idea. "I don't want you doing something that might be dangerous," she insisted.

"Mom, I'm almost fourteen!" Joe objected. He thought for a moment, trying to come up with a better argument. "Look, what if you come along, too? And maybe Sam could ask her dad."

Ellen raised an eyebrow. "This is important to you, isn't it?"

Joe nodded, sensing that she was beginning to waver. "Yes."

With a sigh, Ellen said, "Let me call Walter and see what he says."

Sam's dad said yes.

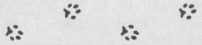

That evening, Ellen, Walter Kepler, Joe, Sam, and David—and, of course, Wishbone—trooped over to Rendezvous Books, armed with sleeping bags and flashlights.

Joe decided that the best place to hide would be behind the ancient oak counter that housed the store's antique cash register. That way, he pointed out, the phone would be right at hand.

"It's sort of a slumber party," Sam said, as they tossed cushions and some thick blankets down to sit on.

Feeling that slumber parties were for giggly little girls, Joe said, "It's more like a stake-out!"

Wishbone looked up sharply, as if wondering where the steak was. In fact, they had no steaks, but Mr. Gurney, who had let them into the store, had laid in a supply of snacks—chips, bananas, cupcakes, sodas, and a bag of Burger Barn burgers, the special ones with both Swiss *and* American cheese. He even brought a small bag of gourmet dog biscuits for Wishbone. They switched the lights off and used a small battery lantern to give them a little dim illumination. Joe thought it was a good substitute for a campfire.

They talked for hours. Finally, Joe began to yawn, feeling his eyelids growing heavy. The old railroad clock on the wall above the counter was ticking on close to one o'clock. Mr. Gurney regaled them with his seemingly inexhaustible supply of ghost stories. He knew a lot of good ones. Mr. Kepler laughed and joined in with some corny jokes, and Ellen tried a few riddles that no one could guess. It was funny, Joe thought, but the adults even seemed like kids again as they told stories, laughed at terrible jokes, or ruffled Wishbone's ears. *Kids have been doing the same things in Oakdale ever since there was an Oakdale,* Joe thought sleepily. It was somehow a comforting idea.

Everyone began to catch the yawns from Joe. "I don't think anyone's gonna show up," David whispered during a lull in the storytelling.

"I'm afraid young David's right, my friends." Mr. Gurney sighed as he leaned back into a comfortable pile of chair cushions. "This has been fun, and it was a good idea, Joe, but I think we're just going to have to admit—"

Then suddenly Wishbone sat up, every fiber of his compact body vibrating. Joe didn't even have to wonder about what Wishbone had heard. He knew what it was. From the abrupt silence, he knew everyone else knew, too. Mr. Gurney switched off the dim lantern, and the darkness dropped like a curtain.

Down below on the first floor, someone had slipped a key into the lock of the alley door, and was slowly opening the back door to Rosie's Rendezvous.

Chapter Twelve

With courage swelling within him, Wishbone perked up his ears even more. His eyes never moved from the door to the landing. "All right, pal, I know you're out there! Give it up to the Official Bookstore Dog, you burglar!" Wishbone began barking.

Joe clamped a hand over Wishbone's muzzle and pulled him back into the darkness behind the counter. "Quiet, boy, quiet!" He held his dog close to his chest.

Wishbone squirmed. "That's easy for you to say, Joe! Your watchdog ancestors aren't crying out for action! Wait a minute! The suspect's getting closer!"

"Mr. Gurney," Walter Kepler whispered, "does anyone besides you, Mary, and the owners of Rosie's have a key to the building?"

Mr. Gurney shook his head.

Whoever had unlocked the back door was now climbing the staircase. Soft footsteps paused on the landing.

He's right outside the door, Wishbone thought.

"It's kids, right?" Sam whispered in a shaky voice. "Just kids—right, Dad?"

The soft footsteps moved again. Wishbone could hear the old doorknob being slowly turned. Then the ancient door opened with a faint whisper of complaint.

"Doesn't sound like a kid," Mr. Kepler muttered under his breath.

The door ghosted open and a tall, lean figure slipped into the bookstore.

Wishbone blinked through the darkness. "And it sure doesn't *look* like a kid."

The dark figure stood framed by the faint light from the open door. It didn't make a sound, but they could see its head moving from side to side, scanning the towering bookcases. It held something bulky.

Wishbone wiggled until he'd slipped his nose free of Joe's grasp. He took a deep sniff. "Books! He's got books, Joe! It's the Reverse Bookstore Burglar for sure!"

Seeming satisfied that everything was all right, the figure turned, hefted its burden, and strode purposefully down one of the aisles. A faint light, like the glow of a

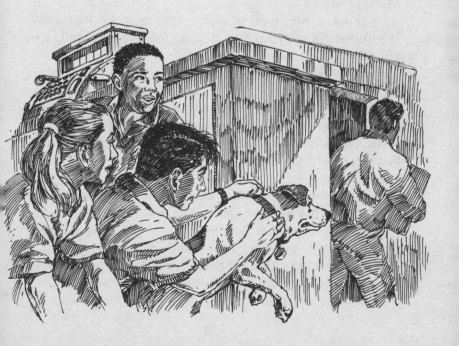

flashlight, appeared in the back of the store. Then the footsteps stopped. The group at the front of the shop could all hear the soft sounds of books being carefully removed from shelves and stacked on the floor. Everyone breathed a sigh of relief. . . .

Except for Wishbone. "It's him! Come on Joe, unleash the Official Bookstore Dog! It's my destiny!"

Silently, Joe slipped over to his employer, who sat stunned on his stack of borrowed cushions. "It's a grown-up, Mr. Gurney! We have to call the police!"

Mr. Kepler reached for the phone. "Ellen, you call, and I'll go see if—"

Wishbone couldn't stand the tension any longer. He squirmed out of Joe's grip. "All right, that's it, time for action!"

Joe made a grab for him, but Wishbone dashed out of his reach.

"Follow me, Joe! *Woo-cha!* Let's get the bad guy!" Wishbone didn't run, but he padded softly ahead, just out of reach.

In Wishbone's opinion, humans were pretty good for most things. In a case like this, however, it was always good to have a little non-human backup. And except for himself, there was only one non-human in the building. Wishbone slipped silently through the rows of crowded bookcases until he reached the chess area . . . and Mr. Faulkner.

The old parrot was asleep. *Or dead,* Wishbone thought, with a distinct lack of charity. He looked up the tall pole upon which Mr. Faulkner sat, his dusty head slumped down between his shoulders. Well, what if Joe did like the ornery green feather-duster? That didn't make Joe any less a friend to Wishbone. And even feather-dusters had their uses!

Wishbone approached the perch. "Sorry about this, bird, but an Official Bookstore Dog's gotta do what an Official Bookstore Dog's gotta do."

He waited until his sharp ears picked up the soft footsteps of the burglar heading back toward the door—and Joe! Wishbone took a deep breath. Then he barked the loudest bark ever barked by a Jack Russell terrier.

"Hey, Mr. Faulkner! *Wake up!* We need all the help we can get!"

There was a loud gasp from the direction of the door. Mr. Faulkner, his voice raised in indignant rage, immediately drowned it out. "Awk! Write what you know! Awk! Write what you know!"

He rose up in the air like an arthritic phoenix, a mythical bird with wings of flame. He began beating the air. Then he swooped.

Wishbone went running back toward the sales counter. "Now, Joe, now! Take a hint! Now!"

Joe took the hint. There was a sharp click, and the overhead lights blazed on. In the naked glare, the figure of Jack Brisco stood blinking, just as a screaming Mr. Faulkner came sailing at him.

"Awk! Write what you know!"

Jack ducked, and the elderly parrot missed him by inches, gliding over to Current Events.

Mr. Faulkner landed with a flutter on top of one of the shelves and screeched, "Pretty bird! Pretty bird!"

Wishbone charged toward the huddled figure of Jack Brisco. The man seemed to be fumbling for something. Then he reared back.

He had taken a few precious seconds to put on his sunglasses.

He turned and lunged for the door, but Wishbone was right behind him and clamped his teeth on the

cuff of one of his black pant legs. "I dot him! I dot him, Doe!"

Jack Brisco limped toward the safety of the door, dragging one determined, squirming Official Bookstore Dog along with him. "Dere's anodder one, Doe! Oudside! Anodder one!"

Wishbone held on for dear life, because he had heard something the humans couldn't—something that could ruin everything!

It was the sound of a second pair of shoes coming up the stairs from Rosie's Rendezvous—far too early to be a policeman reacting to Ellen's phone call. Everyone was coming out of hiding, and he couldn't warn them without letting the burglar get away!

Then a quiet voice spoke from the dark of the landing. "It's all right, Jack. We're caught."

And Dr. Quentin Quarrel stepped into the room.

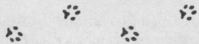

Joe held Wishbone, amazed at how his plan had turned out. They were all in the chess corner now. Dr. Quarrel was sitting, and Jack Brisco standing protectively over him. Ellen had not made the call to the police— everything had happened so fast that she hadn't had time to react. Now the two culprits didn't look very dangerous at all, so the others just waited for an explanation.

Mr. Gurney asked, "Why, Quentin? Why?"

Dr. Quarrel sat slumped in one of the old overstuffed chairs, his head in his hands. He looked drained. Jack Brisco put his hand on the old man's shoulder. Wishbone, Mr. Gurney, Ellen, Mr. Kepler, Joe, Sam, and David stood facing the pair.

Mr. Faulkner, for some reason known only to himself,

131

had decided he wanted to settle on Mr. Gurney's shoulder, making the bookstore owner look somewhat like an elderly pirate. Occasionally, Mr. Faulkner would mutter a dark "Write what you know!" Sometimes he followed up with "Pretty bird!"

Finally, Jack Brisco sighed. "You're going to have to tell him, Grampa." He took his dark glasses off and tucked them back in his jacket pocket. "At least I won't have to wear these stupid glasses anymore."

"*Grampa?*" Mr. Gurney sputtered. Joe looked from Dr. Quarrel to Jack Brisco. For the first time, he noticed the two of them were identically tall and thin.

Dr. Quarrel looked up at his friend and shook his head sadly. Slowly, he got up from the chair, until he stood straight and tall next to Jack Brisco. They both looked at Mr. Gurney and the kids.

Now that both tall men were standing, Joe could really see the strong family resemblance they shared. "Wow!" he said, looking from one to the other.

"I'll be bound up in a leather folio and put on the shelf marked 'Moron'!" Mr. Gurney said, then gasped.

They stood side by side, young and old; two tall, lean, dark men with slicked-back hair and sharp noses. They smiled and their white teeth flashed. But that wasn't the real giveaway, not in Joe's opinion. The clincher was Dr. Quarrel's startling blue eyes staring at them out of Jack Brisco's face.

"That's why you wore the glasses!" Sam said.

Jack nodded at her and sighed.

Blinking, Mr. Gurney spread his hands. "But . . . but . . . but—"

"Oh, stop sputtering, Kilgore," Dr. Quarrel said in a tired voice, as he settled back into his chair. "You look like a landed trout."

Mr. Brisco said, "I thought this was too outrageous to begin with, but I like my grandfather, and he wanted to go through with it." He turned to Dr. Quarrel and warned, "Tell them the whole truth, Grampa, or I will."

With a sigh, Dr. Quarrel said, "All right, all right. How long have we known each other, Kilgore?"

Mr. Gurney shook his head, making the parrot do a fast sideways shuffle. "What? Oh, ten years—ever since you moved to Oakdale after you retired from the state university. Why?"

"Did I ever tell you that I got my undergraduate degree from Oakdale College? Or that I used to know your father?"

Now it was Mr. Gurney's turn to sink down into a chair. Joe thought the old man looked as if someone had just punched him in the stomach.

Dr. Quarrel continued. "It was during the Great Depression. Oakdale College had a special work-study program. If a student could pass the entrance exams but was too poor to pay the tuition, the student could work at the school. The program provided a room in one of the dorms and a meal ticket, but that was all. No money for buying books."

Joe began to get a glimmer of what must have gone on. "Mr. Gurney's father ran the college bookstore back then," he said.

Dr. Quarrel nodded. "Exactly right, Joe. Kilgore's father used to let me hang around the campus bookstore. He was a very nice man—a lot like you, Kilgore. And I repaid him for his kindness by stealing the books I needed."

Mr. Gurney blinked at his friend. "Oh, Quentin—"

Holding up his hand, Dr. Quarrel said softly, "Let me finish. He'd have probably given me the books if I'd asked, but I had too much pride. Then I graduated and went off to fight in the war. When I got back, I finished my education. For years, my thefts preyed on my mind. Then I retired and moved back to Oakdale. And you became my friend. I wanted to pay back the Gurneys—with interest—because I knew the store could use some extra money. But I couldn't bring myself to confess, and I knew you wouldn't just take the money."

Mr. Gurney nodded. "I remember. Once you asked if you could invest in the store."

"And you refused because you said investments could be risky. That's when I remembered *The Haunted Bookshop*."

The mention of the title made Joe's heart beat a little faster. "You read that book, too?" he asked.

Dr. Quarrel nodded. "Oh, certainly. I always liked

Christopher Morley. He was a great Sherlock Holmes expert, you know."

"That's where I came into this whole scheme," Jack Brisco said, taking up the story from his grandfather. "I really do deal in rare books. Grampa had inherited some money. He had me put together a pile of books from my own inventory. Then he gave me a key to the back door and told me where everything was. I was supposed to 'plant' the books where they could be found, and then 'buy' them with Grampa's money."

"But why did you have to knock all the books around?" Joe asked, still puzzled. "Why didn't you just leave the books and let Dr. Quarrel find them?"

Jack Brisco threw back his head and laughed. "That was *my* question! I told Grampa he was making everything too complicated. At first, I was just going to sneak around after hours and scatter the books through the store, but you nearly caught me."

Joe understood at once. "So that was you hiding up here on my first day of work. I wondered about that."

With an embarrassed smile, Jack said, "Yes, I was the mysterious intruder. If it's any comfort, Joe, you scared the wits out of me. I didn't realize that you hadn't left with Mr. Gurney, and I came out of hiding too soon. I had to run for it!"

"You scared me, too," admitted Joe, relieved to know that he hadn't faced a real burglar. "So, after that, you decided to break into the store and leave the books?"

Jack pointed to Dr. Quarrel. "It was Grampa's idea, not mine. He had me break a basement window to cover up the fact that he had a key. Then afterward he felt really guilty about breaking the window, so I never did it again."

Ellen, Joe, and Mr. Kepler exchanged glances. Joe

asked what he thought they all had been wondering: "Where did you get the key?"

Dr. Quarrel shrugged. "I borrowed it from under the sales counter one afternoon when our chess game broke up. I walked down to the hardware store and had it duplicated. Then I brought it back here without Kilgore even suspecting it had been taken!"

Mr. Kepler sighed. "This whole scheme seems too complicated for me!"

With a chuckle, Jack said, "Grampa loves complications! You should see the way he plays chess. His plot wouldn't have been any fun if it hadn't been tricky and convoluted!"

"So, now you know the whole story, Kilgore," Dr. Quarrel said, unable to look at his friend. "It was partly a way to pay you back for what I did to your father, and partly a stupid game. I'm sorry."

For a few moments, Mr. Gurney sat in his chair, his mouth still hanging open. Finally, he shut it with a snap and rose slowly to his feet.

"Quentin Quarrel," he said sternly, "you are an old fool. You are irritable and quarrelsome and opinionated and smug—and you cheat at chess!" Dr. Quarrel bowed his head as Mr. Gurney thundered on. "Of all the idiotic enterprises I have ever heard of—or read about—*this* takes the cake."

"Now, just a minute, Mr. Gurney—" Jack Brisco started to say.

"You be quiet, young man! I am speaking to your massively misguided grandfather! I am shocked—do you hear me, shocked! I am so shocked that I am afraid that I am going to have to ask you to . . . to . . . live up to your offer, invest in the store, and accept a position here as my partner."

Everyone gaped at Mr. Gurney, especially Dr. Quarrel. He sat there with his mouth wide open.

Mr. Gurney roared. "Oh, your face, your face! Who looks like a landed trout now, Quentin! Oh, the look on your face!" And he laughed long and loud.

"You mean that you forgive me?" Dr. Quarrel asked nervously, as soon as Mr. Gurney subsided to gasps and giggles.

"Of course I forgive you, you fussy old fossil! How could I possibly be mad at someone who would go to all this trouble to lend me money! I'm sure I never mentioned my sister Dorothy to you, or how much she and I loved *The Wonderful Wizard of Oz*, but your trick brought it all back. Besides, if I didn't forgive you, I'd probably be up to my neck in Gutenberg Bibles and Shakespeare First Folios!"

"No, you wouldn't," Jack Brisco said, slapping his stunned grandfather on the back. "I don't have any."

Finally, even Dr. Quarrel started laughing, and soon the entire bookstore shook as everyone joined in.

Mr. Faulkner, who didn't seem to appreciate a good burst of laughter, fluttered back to his perch, squawked a couple of times, then went to sleep.

"I assume you are accepting my offer of partnership in Rendezvous Books?" Mr. Gurney said at last, wiping tears of joy from his eyes.

Dr. Quarrel shook his hand. "Of course I accept, you elderly bibliophile! It's what I wanted all along."

Clapping his friend on the back, Mr. Gurney said, "I thought you might! Say, we have all these snacks and sodas and things—don't want it to go to waste . . . or to your waist. Why don't the two of you join us for a little refreshment?"

"We'd love to," Dr. Quarrel said teasingly. "There's

only one thing I regret. The young lady Jack is dating, Mary Benson, is not here to join us."

"Grampa," warned Jack Brisco.

"I'm not thinking of you," Dr. Quarrel told him sternly. "For your information, Mary Benson is a cheerful young lady whose conversation I enjoy, and, more important—she has the only key to the vending room! I'd like a soda right now!"

Grinning, Joe went behind the counter and opened the cooler. "I can take care of that," he said.

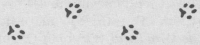

A satisfied Wishbone lay curled up under Mr. Faulkner's perch and watched the party that grew out of the Great Burglary Stake-Out. Just above him, he could hear Mr. Faulkner's rasping snores. "You've got the right idea, bird. A nap would be just the thing right now." He settled his head down on his paws and yawned. "You know, Mr. Faulkner, you're not so bad, after all. I don't even mind if Joe pets you a little."

The sleeping parrot did not respond. Still feeling pleased with his accomplishment, the Official Bookstore Dog of Rendezvous Books chuckled to himself as he went to sleep.

And that ended it—almost. At last the party broke up. Mr. Kepler drove David, Joe, Ellen, and Wishbone home. It was nearly three in the morning, and Joe was dog-tired as he climbed out of the car, his legs feeling clumsy because of his exhaustion. As soon as Joe opened the front door, Wishbone padded upstairs, while Joe and Ellen thanked Sam and her dad for all of their help.

"You'd better go to bed, Joe," Ellen said as they entered the house.

Joe yawned until his mouth felt as though it would stick open. With an effort, he closed it. "I'm heading upstairs right now," he promised.

He got to his room and found Wishbone already curled up on the bed. Joe reached to ruffle his buddy's ears and give him a soothing scratch.

"Well, everything turned out for the best," Joe said, pulling off his shirt. He was about to toss it in the corner when something caught his eye. He dropped the shirt and went to the other side of the bed.

Joe picked up the battered copy of *The Haunted Bookshop* from his bedside table. It felt good in his hands, compact and solid. He liked the way the story had ended, although the climactic bomb blast had damaged the bookstore and had a sad impact on some of the characters' lives. Still, life had gone on, and the bad guys had been beaten.

Holding the book, Joe thought again about all the kids of Oakdale over the years: a ten-year-old Mr. Gurney reading *The Wonderful Wizard of Oz* to his little sister, Dorothy; his mom wrapped up in one of the nurse novels she had told him she used to love; a young Stevie Talbot, trying to solve the mystery of the haunted bookshop, just the way Joe had done.

Pausing a moment with the book in his hand, Joe smiled. Then he said softly, "We did it together. Good night, Dad." And he put the book on his own shelf. It looked right at home.

About Brad Strickland

Brad Strickland has written two books from The Adventures of Wishbone series, *Be a Wolf!* and *Salty Dog*, and has collaborated with Thomas E. Fuller on another book from the WISHBONE Mysteries series, *The Treasure of Skeleton Reef*. He has also written many short stories, along with twenty novels for adults and for younger readers, including five books in the popular mystery series that was begun by the late John Bellairs. He also collects books—not rare editions, but lots and lots of titles that he loves to read.

Brad teaches English at Gainesville College in Gainesville, Georgia. He and his wife, Barbara, have two children, Amy and Jonathan. They also have a houseful of pets, including a bunny, ferrets, cats, and two dogs, who resemble Wishbone only in their enthusiasm for digging holes in the yard.

About Thomas E. Fuller

In addition to writing WISHBONE books, Thomas E. Fuller is the head writer of the Atlanta Radio Theatre, a playwright, and a screenwriter. Thomas has written many exciting radio dramas, and his stage plays have been performed all over the country. His expertise in rare and used books gave him the idea for the plot of *Riddle of the Wayward Books*. The combination of a lively, funny dog and lovely old books was just too good to resist. He and Brad Strickland have collaborated on another WISHBONE mystery, *The Treasure of Skeleton Reef*, as well as a number of short stories, radio plays, and other work.

Thomas and his wife, Berta, live in Duluth, Georgia, with their children (all Wishbone fans), Christina, John, Anthony, and Edward. When he's not writing, Thomas and his family enjoy seaside vacations, science-fiction conventions, and cruising the Internet.